All Kinds of Everything

All Kinds of Everything

Short Stories, Poems and Memories from SWit'CH

Copyright and Ordering

First Printing: 2023
ISBN: 9798371732019

Swinton Writers in t'Critchley Hub

A community-based assembly of creative writers based around Swinton in Salford, Lancs, UK
Founded in 2015 at Age UK, Swinton Community Hub
Member of The National Association of Writers Groups UK.

Ordering Information:

Published with Amazon KDP. Available through Amazon and good book distributors or directly from us.

E-mail: switchswinton@gmail.com

Contents

Fading

Then, when you knew who I am
When you were young
And beautiful
Was it only yesterday
You'd laugh and sing
Around the house.
When was it that
The black cloud appeared
Obscuring the memory
Of all you knew.
Now, you look at me
Through vacant eyes
Wondering, who is this
Stranger staring back at you
But I know you!

I wonder what goes on
Behind that vacant stare
Sometimes I sing to you
You sing along with me
Strange how you remember songs
But don't remember me
But I remember you
I will always remember you
My beautiful sister, who
Can never know the sadness,
The heartbreak of
Knowing that we will never again
Know the joy of shared memories
Of younger days
Precious memories I still have
Now denied to you

You are here in front of me
But a million miles away
In your own little world
I can only hope that you
Are happy there. You laugh a lot
At things I can't see
And so, I have to be content
With the smiling face I see
I laugh and sing with you
Then when I leave you there
My heart breaks anew
For that beautiful girl
Without a care in the world
Now you don't have a care
In the world, for
That world is lost to you
The world as you knew it then
Before the black cloud came
To hide that world from you
To hide you away from me

Though you no longer know
Who I am
I remember who you were
Who you still are to me
I know you!
I will always remember you!
You may not remember
Who you were, but

I will remember you for you.

MARY YOUNG

A Garden Mystery

BARBARA SHEARWOOD

Mrs Winthrop was peering out of her window and my husband Frank muttered, "That nosy old bat is there again, has she got nothing better to do?"

I said, "Oh Frank, perhaps she doesn't have anything better to do. She's all alone now since her husband died and I don't think she ever has any visitors. I've never seen people calling on her, anyway."

"Yes, well," he muttered, "she just puts me off doing any jobs outside with her watching all the time."

"Well that's a new excuse," I said, "I thought you were going to weed the front garden this week and it is Thursday already."

Okay," he grumbled, "I'll do it now, anything for a quiet life."

I went into the kitchen to make some scones ready for my friend Jenny who was coming to see me that afternoon. When I'd put them in the oven I went to look out of the front window to see how Frank was getting on with the weeding. He was there with a rake in his hand, but it didn't look as though he had done much actual weeding. I hid behind the curtain so he wouldn't see me and I glanced across the road. I could see Mrs Winthrop apparently watching him. "At this rate he'll be there all day," I thought.

I went back into the kitchen and took the scones out of the oven. They looked perfect. They would be just the thing for my get-together with Jenny later.

I went back again to see how Frank was getting on, but he wasn't there and Mrs Winthrop was not in her window either. So I went outside to see where he was. I looked all around the garden and in the shed, but I couldn't find him anywhere.

A few minutes later he rushed in through the back door.

"Where have you been?" I asked him, "I've been outside and in the shed looking for you, but you weren't there."

"No, I've been across the road at Mrs Winthrop's. She came over to me while I was in the garden and she asked if I knew of any local gardeners who could do a heavy job for her. So I went over to see what she wanted doing. She explained that when they had moved into their house there was a big rockery in the back garden. That was fine when her husband was alive, but she couldn't manage it now, so she wanted to get all the rocks removed so she could have the lawn extended. She kept saying she would pay for it to be done if she could find someone reliable. I could see that some of the rocks were quite big so I said I would do it for her. She asked me how much it would cost, but I felt sorry for the old dear and I said I would do it for nothing. So tomorrow morning I am going to go across and see what I can do. Well I'd better get on with my weeding, hadn't I? Or you'll be on at me again about getting my own jobs done."

So out he went just as Jenny arrived. We had a nice cup of tea and she enjoyed my scones and we chatted about the people we used to work with. She told me about Jane from the accounts department who now has twin grandchildren and Mary, the assistant secretary who has been promoted. She is now the manager in what used to be my department. It was lovely to hear all her news, but I'm glad I've retired now.

She was just putting her coat on to leave when Frank came in and said he'd finished the weeding and wanted a rest. When Jenny had gone I looked at the spare scones I had and I thought about poor Mrs Winthrop, sitting there all alone, so I put a couple in a bag and took them over to her. She was quite overcome but I said I'd made too many and I didn't want to put them out for the birds. It was the first time I'd really chatted to her but I've decided it won't be the last.

Well the next morning Frank went over to see what he could do about moving the rockery stones. He was there ages, but later he rushed into the house and said,

"I've got to make a phone call. I think it had better be to the police."

"Why, what do you mean?" I asked, "Is Mrs Winthrop alright? Does she need an ambulance?"

"No, she's fine, but I've just dug up one of the big stones in her back garden and there's a skeleton under it!"

So that's what he did and he explained that it looked very old and he wasn't sure who to contact. Later a Police car came and two policemen went round into Mrs Winthrop's back garden. A few minutes later another police vehicle arrived and several officers wearing hazard suits and masks and gloves went round the back! It was just like CSI on the telly! I must say I was very curious and wanted to know what was going on, but I thought I'd better keep out of the way

5

Well the upshot of all this was that the remains were very old so the police informed the university. A couple of days later a professor and some students came and started digging to see if anything else was buried there.

They did remove the skeleton and they took it back to the university to be tested to see how old it was. Well that was that for a while, but the students are back again now and they are doing more digging. Mrs Winthrop is in her element, making them cups of tea and snacks all the time. She doesn't have time now to stand at her front window looking out. I see more of her now and we've become really friendly, so when the students are not there we have many a good gossip.

I said to her the other day, "No-one expected to come across a body in a suburban back garden, did they?"

"Not a body," she corrected me, "a skeleton!"

Well that does make a difference, doesn't it? She is a bit of a perfectionist with her use of language, but then she was a teacher of English at our local High School, so she does know what she's talking about.

Also the university have decided that the skeleton was probably a plague victim from the mid sixteen hundreds and that there used to be an old burial ground somewhere near here.

I think they are going to do more searches in the area, so who knows what will turn up next?

1968 the Year That Changed My Life

PAULINE MITCHELL

In the Spring of 1968, I met and chatted to a husband and wife couple I met at a Parish Social. (These were held regularly in those days, usually once a month.) The wife was telling me that she had recently started a new career- in teaching. She had already told me she had five small children, and I wondered how on earth she could manage- I had six, aged between three -year-old twins and a ten-year-old, and felt that my hands were full, so naturally hoped for some tips. My qualifications weren't that good, and I didn't think I'd be accepted for college, though I liked children and the teachers' hours and holidays made it seem a good idea.

I knew of course, that there was a desperate shortage of teachers- my little girl was five, and more than ready to begin school, but must wait till September.

So my husband and I discussed the idea, and I had a chat with our children's' headmaster. He told me that a new teacher training college had opened just fifteen miles away, specifically for "mature students". Also, I was learning to drive. The jigsaw was beginning to take shape. I applied to start in September.

I was interviewed by a rather bemused tutor, who wanted me to wait till next year if I wanted to take English as a main subject- that course was full. So I asked which courses were not full. "Physics, Philosophy and International Relations," came the answer "Aha! International Relations!." I had read a newspaper every day since my English teacher recommended that we read *The Observer* every Sunday, (which I still did, along with the *Chronicle* every weekday), To my surprise I was accepted and at that moment everything changed.

The twins, aged three, went to a nursery. I drove them there and either my husband or myself brought them home. The others were all at the same primary school, so the logistics were simple and effective. I relished the freedom and the mental stimulus of study, and felt more alive and energised by the challenges, mental, physical and social, of learning in an atmosphere so much more informal than my own schooling.

It also brought me to a realisation that I was capable of becoming a better mother, more understanding wife, and perhaps cleverer than I had thought myself. But my area of comparison had shifted- my younger sister had always been "The Clever One", focused from very early in life on becoming a lawyer, going to University and "Doing Well." My aspirations had been much more modest, and I realised that here was something I could be good at. Not glamorous, not going to University, but with a professional qualification that I could build on, which was useful to me, my family and the people I taught and understood. I loved it!

And I had the confidence to continue to study from my retirement from full time work at 55, until the age of 83, with degrees in Counselling and Ancient History. It's all about confidence and the steadfast support of husband and children.

Actions Speak Louder than Words.

PAUL MULDOON

Nokia Tone: De De Der De ----- De De Der De-

Girlfriend	Hello Dazza! What you calling for at this time? You're working, aren't ya?
Darren	Yeah, Babe. I'm working on a property in the town centre and called into that cafe for lunch, you know the one...'
Girlfriend	Yeah, the one you insist on using as often as possible. Miss micro mini, low-cut top and big boobs.'
Darren	Kylie.'
Girlfriend	Yeah, that's her name – it's a wonder you ever noticed her name badge, come to think of it, it's a wonder she had anywhere to pin it to!'
Darren	Look, I didn't phone you up for an argument, something's kicking off in here, that's why I'm calling.'
Girlfriend	What is it? What is it?'
Darren	There's a couple sat near me and I think they're having a barney.'
Girlfriend	What do you mean, *think*?' They either are, or they're not!'
Darren	Let me explain. I think they're deaf and dumb, they're using sign language.'
Girlfriend	So, if they're not making any sound, how do you know they're having a barney?'

Darren	They're both signing at the same time, it's all very frantic and I know body language when I see it!'
Girlfriend	Well, what do you think they're saying?'
Darren	She's holding her heart and pointing at him. Now she's pointing at Kylie and holding her hands over her eyes.'
Girlfrien	'Oh, I see, I see, Darren, he's just like you, can't keep his eyes off the tart.'
Darren	No! There's more to it than that, I'm sure. Oh! Something's happening!'
Girlfriend	What is it? What is it?'
Darren	She's pulling at her finger, she's pulling the ring off her finger! Oh, it's off and she's flung it at him. It's fell on the floor! He's looking for it, oh! He's found it and stood up again. Oh, no! Now that sign I *did* understand!'
Girlfriend	What did he do? What did he do?'
Darren	He stuck two fingers up at her. Oh, no! It's just got worse!'
Girlfriend	What's happening, Dazza? What's happening, Dazza?'
Darren	She's flung her milkshake all over him!'
Girlfriend	Oh, no!'
Darren	He's going out. I think that in radio-speak is what you might call over and out.'
Girlfriend	It's not fair to make a joke about it, Dazza, she'll be upset.'

Darren	She is! She is! Her head's in her hands, I think she must be crying. Kylie's come over and put her arms round her... Oh, no!'
Girlfriend	What's happened? What's happened?'
Darren	She looked up and saw it was Kylie's arm and shrugged her away... Kylie's slipped on the milkshake and fell over... I'd better go and help.'
Girlfriend	Darren! Darren! Don't get involved, it's none of your business!'
Darren	Okay, Babe, catch you up later, bye!' ... 'Here, let me help you, Kylie.'
Kylie	Oh, thanks. It's Darren, isn't it?'
Darren:	Yeah , that's right.'
Kylie	My knight in shining armour!'

Lessons will be Learned

"Lessons will be learned
It just won't happen again."
They Won't. It will.
Until they explain –
Why?
A conspiracy of corruption
A cartel of collusion.
Infects and infests
Each institution –
That turns
A blind eye;
That tilts
A deaf ear;
All arses are covered
To save their career.
Where!
Silence is bought
Scruples are sold;
Pay, perks and pensions
Are guarded like gold;
No one is punished
No one dismissed;
No one is given
A slap on the wrist
So!
"Lessons will be learned
It won't happen again"
They won't. it will.
And they'll still remain...

WARREN DAVIES

In a Cell (Trapped)

PAUL HALLOWS

A single moonbeam shone down on this ghastly room. Dark and dingy. It illuminated a spot on the wall while I'm huddled in this rat-infested swamp. Another day in hell. Trapped in a prison cell.

Clunk, click, the door is open.

'Get ready Miller. Another day. Get up.'

I hadn't slept a wink. Another tear rolls down my face. I brush it aside. Don't want them to see me cry. Come on, be strong Miller, I told myself.

Some say prisoners have a life of luxury, TV, PlayStation. Home from home. This is far from the truth.

Led to the kitchen area to get my food. Meatballs in gravy. Didn't matter if you liked it or not. Food. Something to eat.

Back to the cell. Just about to eat my food when one of the prison guards barges in and throws my food everywhere. Two more come in and lock the door then proceed to beat me up. They start to laugh as they exit the door.

Clunk, click. Door closed again. I'm on my own.

The shutter on the door is pulled down. One of the officers glances in. Clunk, click, door opened. He hands me a broom. 'Come on, Miller. Tidy your cell.'

'But it wasn't my fault!' I said. Needn't have bothered. Fell on deaf ears.

After I cleaned up. I glanced outside the cell. The two officers that beat me up were going by, looking at me and laughing.

Clunk, click. Door closed again. I'm on my own.

Looking out of the window I notice it's raining, each drop of rain playing a symphony of pain that I can relate to. I snuggle down on my bed. Terrified of what will happen next.

Yesterday they had dragged me across the floor by my arms and then proceeded to throw buckets of water onto me. When the boss man asked, 'What's happened?' the officers said, 'Oh, he's wet himself again,' and then laughed.

The shrieks of laughter echo in my mind. Why can't they just let me be?

The only comfort is the light underneath the door. One day I will be free, I think to myself. Maybe a dream, but that's helping me cope with it all.

I've not had a shower for weeks. Must really stink now.

Officers must have read my mind.

Clunk, click.

They take me for a shower. It feels great to get a shower if only to get a moment from the wretched cell. I let the water flow over me as I get a wash down. Shower off, back into prison attire and once again back to the cell.

I hear Harvey in the next cell screaming in pain. God knows what they are doing to him. Poor bloke. He was always good to me. Probably the only friend I have got here.

Got a new pet today. A little mouse I found in my cell. Called him 'Mr Bojangles,' like the song. Managed to get a meal today. Anything left went to Mr Bojangles.

Managed to get some sleep tonight for the first time. Mr Bojangles came at the right time as I was thinking of giving up. He has helped me to cope with it all.

Clunk, click. Door opened. Brand new day.

Days seem the same in here. Nothing different, I couldn't tell you what day it was, or time.

Mr Bojangles ran away out of my cell.

'Hey!' I said to the officer, 'Get Mr Bojangles for me.'

'What?' said the officer.

'Get my mouse for me?' I shouted.

'Oh, I see,' he replied. Then proceeds to stamp on its head till it's dead.

'Noooo!' I screamed. 'What harm has he done to you? You cruel person!'

Tears streamed down my face. My little friend. DEAD.

Clunk, click. Door closed again.

How can you kill a little mouse? I thought. My little friend.

Silence.

What will tomorrow bring?

Rainbows

When the rain is hammering,
And you cannot see,
Beyond your tears.

When the thunder's deafening
And its sound reminds,
You of your fears.

Have faith!

There will be a rainbow,
Hidden somewhere deep,
Amongst the grey.

Bright colours set to paint,
Over the darkness,
To light your day.

Look up - smile!

Let colours warm your heart,
Feel them gently float
Your cares away.

Then, when clouds reform, your
Own rainbow of hope,
Will point the way.

SYLVIA EDWARDS

John McNulty's Dead.

JUDITH BARRIE

'The way John would pass an exam was by cheating. That's how he got into MI5, you know.'

'I didn't know that,' I said. Although I did.

Pamela Hutchinson was what you would call a 'nice lady'. I felt sorry for her; she'd been genuinely very fond of John, the copious tears at the funeral had been real. And close enough to him that he could tell her he was in MI5. But here we were, three vodka martinis in and she was opening up nicely.

'John wasn't his real name, you know.'

Of course I knew, but simply nodded sympathetically and let her run on.

'No. His real name was Gregory. Gregory Fairbank, but he told me they thought it sounded a bit too Russian.' She laughed, nervously.

'Mm.' I leaned in closer. 'I can see the point.'

She drained her glass. 'Oh,' she said, something dawning on her, 'I suppose your real name isn't Ian, is it?'

'Well, yes it is. This is the *real* me today. And am I getting the *real* Pamela?' I asked, managing a flirty laugh. 'Another drink?'

She didn't answer, but I got up and went to the bar anyway.

A funeral is the best place to hide in plain sight. Back at the house half the guests had been relatives and the other half work colleagues, ex-girlfriends and all manner of casual acquaintances and the one half didn't have a clue about the other. Pamela Hutchinson had been easy to spot, on her own, looking lost, clutching the martini glass. And besides, I knew what she looked like, I'd seen her picture in our files.

She'd been *very* close to John for a *very* long time, staying around after their mad fling twenty years before as his bezzie mate, so at the house after the short service at the crematorium, I made a beeline for her.

'Hi.' I said softly, 'I think you must be Pamela.'

She looked up at me a bit dazed, her mascara slightly smudged where she'd rubbed at the tears.

'John showed me a photograph of you, oh, it must have been years ago. He used to talk about you, often.'

She wasn't bad looking, for her age. Immaculately turned out with a short blond hairstyle – it had been much longer in the file pictures. But definitely not my type.

'Oh, sorry! I'm Ian Foster.' She looked at me blankly. 'I worked with John. Sometimes. You know what it was like…'

'Oh, yes. I knew what it was like.'

We were both smiling at each other now, like old friends, or at least that's how I hoped it looked to the spooks who were undoubtedly scanning the crowd.

From then on it was easy-peasy. I knew enough about her to convince her that John and I had had many a cosy chat about her and she was familiar enough with the rules to understand that when she asked: *So what exactly did you work on with John…?* I simply said, 'Sorry, you know I can't discuss…'

'Oh, no, of course not…'

After about twenty minutes of warming her up, I said: 'Look, do you want to get away from this crowd and go somewhere a bit quieter? Somewhere we can have a proper drink away from all this? I know a little place, the Blue Mermaid, perhaps…?'

She went to get her coat and we trotted off like two old chums.

The Blue Mermaid was a bit out of the way to start with, and I went the long way round because I wanted to make sure we'd not been followed. We settled in a secluded corner and I seated her so that she was sitting with her back to the bar – I didn't want her to see the barman pouring me alcohol-free San Miguel. She was very happy with her vodka martinis.

When I brought the first drink back she was dabbing at her eyes again with a tissue.

'Oh, I still can't believe it! He was only fifty-six.' She started to sob.

I put my hand on her arm and stroked it. 'People say it can be a bad age, fifty-six.'

'I mean, I know he'd had trouble with his heart…And he would still smoke, you know…I told him *so* many times…And the drinking…! Sometimes he'd say I was nagging him, but it was only because I cared so much…' More tissues were produced and I moved in even closer, eventually gently stroking her cheek when she'd wiped it dry again.

I said: 'Yes. It's been a great shock to us all. I shall miss him very much.' In fact, I'd never met John McNulty, but they'd needed a fresh face for the job, somebody never seen in the UK before.

It was when she was another twenty minutes in that she started to really open up. God! It was a tedious business sometimes. I don't know why we just didn't drag her in and apply a little persuasion, but then disposing of the body would have been a tiresome nuisance.

'What makes it worse,' she said, 'is the last time I saw him, I hardly gave him the time of day! I'd just flown in to Venice for a couple of weeks and I was meeting up with Bonzer Harris – he was due in on the flight that afternoon at Marco Polo. You must know Bonzer, he was a friend of John's for years.'

That was a new name to remember. I made a mental note.

'Oh, yes,' I said, smiling and nodding. 'Old Bonzer, eh?' More smiling and nodding.

'Well, at the airport I found John in the Terminal Bar and Grill. He was sober for a change, just had an orange juice in front of him! Well, it looked like orange juice. Anyway, he said he was waiting for Fred, Fred Morley. You must know…?'

'Yes, yes, of course.'

'Well, John looked absolutely pee-d off; said he'd been there for nearly two hours and Fred hadn't turned up. I could tell he was *really* annoyed. But then he said something strange, he said, "Don't tell Bonzer why I was here, will you? In fact, Pammy…" That's what he called me. Pammy. "In fact, don't tell him you've seen me at all."

'Well, I did as I was told. Always did. So I met up with Bonzer when the flight came in and off we went, exploring - I wanted to see those wonderful Tintorettos again at the Museo Correr. And I didn't give another thought to what John had said.'

She paused for another sniffle. 'Then I never saw John again after we both got back to England.'

Another pause for a while, then her face crumpled and she started to blub in earnest.

So, if John was in the dark, it seemed unlikely that the Brits had been responsible for Fred's body, found tortured and dumped in the safe house in Croydon. That was blown now. And we hadn't taken out our own best double agent ourselves, so that left CIA. Well, well!

'Well, I knew Fred's wife, you know, Valerie,' a recovered Pam wittered on. 'We did a pottery class together for years, then when that finished we did lunches and played tennis sometimes. She has a killer service.'

Pammy was getting boring now and I had a plane to catch leaving for Moscow in a couple of hours. Time to split.

'Pamela, I'd really like us to meet up again, to have a meal or something. In better circumstances. I have to go back to the office for an hour or two now, so...Could I have your telephone number? And perhaps we can arrange something? In a couple of days?'

I produced my diary and made a show of taking her details. I would check with the files to see if they were genuine. I almost wanted to tell her: *It was very quick, Pam. John hardly suffered at all.* Wonderful new drugs we've got these days, and they don't leave a single trace.

I stood up to leave. 'It's been lovely meeting you Pam. I hope we can see a lot more of each other.'

'Yes. I'd like that,' she slurred. Hopefully she was too drunk to even be able to describe my face.

As I turned, I said: 'I wonder if Fred ever turned up?'

'Oh, no,' she said. 'He never even got to Venice. Valerie said a couple of days before, Fred had gone out to the car wash and never come back...'

Loss

She woke suddenly, the dream gone completely like a door closing.

She listened intently, not even opening her eyes in case the simple muscle movement disturbed her concentration.

A bird song,

distant traffic,

but nothing closer.

She could feel her heart beating faster, sweat on her forehead and armpits.

Slowly her body began to relax.

What time is it?

Her unopened eyes detected that it was no longer dark.

Her mind wondered, what day is it?

Had he got football today?

Would she bring her disruptiveness to the breakfast table?

Then realisation

An unbidden tear.

They were no longer here.

She tried to escape into the lost dream without success,

She listened to her heartbeat,

Wishing it would stop but the steady healthy rhythm tormented her. Gradually she moved one limb after another and opened her eyes.

She looked at the clock and willed herself to get up and get on.

One step at a time.

VERONICA SCOTTON

Green Peppers.

PAUL MULDOON

Charlotte ate green peppers all day long and Barry had had enough of it. He had been left holding the baby, so to speak. His daughter, Anita had moved on from the time of an insistent teenager.

'I want a pet rabbit for my birthday!' and after so many 'No's' her parents had relented and so Charlotte - floppy-eared and with a coat like black velvet – joined the family. That was eight years ago and now Anita had met Paul, they had fallen in love, married and moved into a posh apartment block.

'They don't allow pets, Dad, she'll have to stay here with you.'

'But I don't want it, it's yours!'

'This is her home, this is where she lives,' Anita retorted.

And so the argument was lost, and Barry had to put up with Charlotte eating all the green peppers he could produce in his small greenhouse and then had to buy them in the shops at other times of the year. Not only did she eat green peppers but had also acquired a penchant for some of the flowers in the garden whenever she was allowed out of her hutch, especially the nasturtiums that Barry loved so much. They were his deceased wife's favourites and since she'd died five years earlier, he had kept a patch of them in a corner of the garden as a memorial. It was fitting that Charlotte liked the nasturtiums as it had been on Joy's insistence that Anita should have the pet rabbit for her fifteenth birthday.

Enough was enough, Barry thought. Since Putin's invasion of Ukraine food prices had rocketed and Charlotte was destined for the pot. He would have a few meals of rabbit stew and he could stop buying the bloody green peppers she insisted on chomping on. *Double-good situation,* Barry thought, as George Orwell would have put it: *double-good.*

So Friday was chosen as the execution day, just in time for Sunday dinner. It wasn't a problem for him, being brought up on a Yorkshire farm where his family were often fed game at the table. Rabbit, pigeon, pheasant were always on the menu. His father had taught him how to kill and skin a rabbit. The rabbit punch was delivered and Charlotte fell limp straight away. She was skinned and cleaned, the feet cut off with the idea of making them into lucky charms for some of his gambling mates. He spent Saturday morning binding the rabbit feet with some bright silk thread from Joy's old sewing box, the black fur hidden behind the bright red silk. *Not a bad job, that, Barry*, he said to himself. *A fiver each, that's twenty quid.*

21

His D I Y skills suddenly stopped when the phone rang. It was Anita. Barry had told her the night before about Charlotte's passing in an upsetting phone call: he had found her dead in her hutch on Friday morning and had buried her under the magnolia tree in his beloved garden, something that both Anita and Joy would have approved of.

'Yes, that's great Dad. I can visit her grave anytime then.'

This phone call threw Barry when she asked if she could come over on Sunday to visit Charlotte's resting place and have Sunday dinner.

'Yes, That'll be fine, love.'

'What will you be making?' she asked.

'Er...chicken casserole,' he lied.

'Oh, that will be nice, with some fresh veg from the garden.'

'Yes, of course!'

'I'll bring my new taffeta dress. I bought it for the dancing competition I've entered with Paul, next weekend.'

'That will be nice. See you tomorrow then, love.'

The rabbit stew next day was converted into chicken casserole with the help of a few various additions, a couple of bay leaves from the garden and fennel seeds always make their presence felt, Barry thought as he sprinkled them into the stew. Finally, a few home-grown tomatoes should do the trick, he decided. Which it did, and during dinner there was no mention of rabbit stew. Paul and Anita had no concerns about the food and accepted the free meal of chicken casserole and home-grown vegetables with grateful thanks.

'Let me show you the dancing dress, Dad,' Anita announced after dinner. 'It's in the car. I'll put it on in my old room.'

A few minutes later she entered the room with her bright red taffeta dress fitting perfectly. 'Wow!' exclaimed Barry. 'You look amazing! You're halfway to winning the competition before you start with a dress like that.'

'Thanks, Dad. Let's go and show it to Charlotte at her graveside.'

'Good idea but be careful of that dress out there. One of my Yorkshire white roses fell across the path the other day.' He might have been talking to himself, Anita was just lost in admiration of herself, looking into the full-length mirror on a nearby wall.

Barry had foreseen this scenario and rather than actually digging a hole next to his lovely magnolia had instead just taken a few shovelfuls of soil from his oldest compost heap and laid them on the ground next to the tree. He'd knocked up a cross and written 'Charlotte' on it, then hammered it into the ground next to the compost.

'Aaw, that cross is a nice touch, Dad. Do you like my new dress, Charlotte? I hope so,' Ainita said, bending down to touch the cross, in some way getting Charlotte's approval. On trying to stand again, Anita trod on her dress and fell backwards. She turned quickly and scrambling to get up she caught her dress on a thorn of the white rose her father had warned her about. On gathering her composure to stand up straight again, both her husband and father both looked, first at her, then at each other.

'What?' Anita shouted.

'Your dress, darling, you dress has a small tear in it on your chest,' Paul replied.

'Oh, no! No! No!'

'Don't worry love,' her father said. 'I can fix that. Leave it with me for a few days, you'll see.' Sure enough, it took only a few days to adapt one of the rabbit's foot lucky charms into a brooch.

Since Joy's passing, Barry had had to learn all kinds of new skills, sewing being one of them. 'There,' he thought, 'not only will it bring her luck in the dancing competition, but it will cover up the tear in her dress.'

Cat And Mouse

Paddy was an Irish cat who lived down in the bog

We knew that he was Irish for he thought he was a dog

He couldn't understand the dog next door, it didn't like him

For every time he tried to say hello the dog would bite him

He gave up trying to be friendly to it in the end

He wondered what he'd have to do to find a proper friend

Sad and dismayed all paddy did was mope around the house

Until behind the skirting board he spied a little mouse

The little mouse looked up at him with great big, frightened eyes

When Paddy said hello to him he fainted in surprise

Paddy thought he'd killed him, but when the mouse came round

Paddy was ecstatic at the brand-new friend he'd found

He took him to the alleyway where cats all love to play

But this was a mistake, as Paddy found out on that day

He said, "Hey guys, I've brought a very good friend home for tea"

How was he to know they'd take his words so literally

They quite misunderstood his meaning 'til it was too late

Paddy cried, observing the remains upon the plate

All his friends just laughed at him as he dissolved in tears

They said, "Thanks Paddy" That was the best meal we've had in years"

Paddy couldn't understand how they could be so cruel

But when it was explained to him he felt a proper fool

"A cat can't make friends with a mouse," a wise old friend advised

"But at least the little chap was happy, just before he died.

You just need educating about how cats should behave

So you can come to school with me to learn how to be brave."

But Paddy wasn't listening to what he had to say.

He really didn't want to be a hero anyway.

Paddy missed his little friend, but no one understood.

He knew that he would never find another quite as good

He never quite got over it, and so, when Paddy died

He and his little friend, the mouse, were buried side by side

The moral of this story is as clear as it can be

A cat can't make friends with a mouse, then take him home

For tea!

MARY YOUNG

Not All Gold Glitters.

JUDITH BARRIE

'But how do we know it's not fake?'

'We dinnae, Jimmy,' said Stewart. 'We dinnae know if it's a fake.'

Stewart screwed up his face, deep in contemplation. 'Tell me again, Jimmy, tell me how you found it.'

Stewart usually had to ask Jimmy at least two or three times before he got the full story, and then it was suspect until proven beyond doubt. Sometimes Stewart felt like beating Jimmy across the head with a baseball bat, but you didn't mess with Alistair McDuff's son; not if you wanted to keep a full set of choppers.

It wouldn't be unfair to say, though, that Alistair McDuff was more than a wee bit disappointed with his only son and heir. Jimmy was his firstborn and at the beginning Alistair was delighted – a son to take over his position as crime-lord of Arbermouth, the small town on the coast, a few miles north of Aberdeen. In fact, there were two crime-lords, rival gangs that controlled the flow of drugs and loot for nearly the whole of the eastern seaboard of Scotland, but these days a tentative balance of power had been reached and it was rare for the weaponry to come out, although there were frequent bitter wars of words. The trouble was, as young Jimmy started to grow, it became apparent that when it had come to handing out the brains, Jimmy had been at the back of the queue. The elevator was stuck in the basement; the picnic-basket only had a packet of crisps and half a bottle of pop; the hamster was in the cage but the wheel wasn't turning; Jimmy was singularly lacking in common sense.

In truth, Alistair wasn't much better: although not known for his mental acuity or great oratory, he made up for his lack of brains with brawn a-plenty. He had been known to pick up a twelve-stone man with one hand to toss him over the bridge into the river (plus the concrete weight). Jimmy was scrawny as a wee lad, with a pronounced squint and a worrying tendency to go off picking wild flowers when his dad took him into the forest for rifle practice. And he was ginger. The only one in the family.

After Jimmy, Alistair's luck ran out entirely and five bonny wee lassies followed, and although twelve-year old Brenda was feisty – she had only last week given the milkman a black eye for leaving strawberry yogurt when he'd run out of raspberry – it wasn't the same as having a

26

son to take over the 'business'.

So when Jimmy reached eighteen, in desperation, he was handed into the care of Stewart Cameron, one of Alistair's trusted gang members, for a bit of 'shaping up'. Stewart was noted for his patience: after all, he'd been courting Sheila McDougall for three years and she was known to be a right handful.

'Right. Concentrate, Jimmy.' Stewart said, 'You were walking down the High Street and…'

'I was walking down the High Street…I'd just been to get sausage rolls from Megsons and the man in front of me slipped on a banana skin and nearly went arse over diddies. It all happened sae quick…Next thing I knew, the man got into a car and drove off and it was lying on the floor. So I picked it up. And brought it here.' Jimmy grinned widely. 'Kin I kep it?'

Stewart looked closely at the Rolex watch on the table in front of him. 'Mm.'

'Is it real, Stewie?'

'I'm not sure, Jimmy. And don't call me Stewie!'

'It's a bit broke, but I really like the green colour. Shall I show ma da?'

'No, no, dinnae be a bampot. 'S only the clasp that's loose, but it's not gold or anything. Looks like stainless steel to me, not too special. We need to find out if's it's a fake first. Let me check it out on the internet.'

The range of Rolex watches on the internet was baffling, dozens of them, but Stewart was astounded to see that prices *started* at £13,000! His mouth dropped open when he came to a picture of an identical specimen.

'Well! Jesus and Mary on a tandem! Here's the wee beauty!' He twisted the screen round to show Jimmy. 'A Rolex Day-Date 40. Oyster! White gold wi' a green face! An' if it's not a fake, it's worth thirty-one thousand punds!'

'Well, kin I kep it?'

'Jimmy! If it's real, I'll buy you a green watch if that's what yer want, but this is goin' to Charlie Grier! Right noo!'

Charlie Grier ran the local pawn shop and acted as fence for the McDuff gang, the local expert on everything and anything that could be lifted from a house. Or a shop. Or a vehicle. Or anywhere else. Over thirty years he had 'come to an arrangement' with the local polis, most of them getting at least a luxury holiday abroad once a year from his largesse.

The doorbell jangled loudly as Stewart and Jimmy entered the shop, Charlie liking plenty of warning if he was in the back 'doing a bit of French polishing'.

'Well, if it isnae Stewie Cameron and wee Jimmy! How's ya da, Jimmy?'

'Oh, he's very well, Mister Grier. We've brought you a wa...'

'Right, Jimmy, I'll tell the tale.' Stewart took the watch out of his pocket and placed it on the counter. 'So, Charlie, what do yer make of *that* wee beauty? Oh, and ma name's not Stewie...'

Charlie stood back in shock and threw his hands up. 'Are yer off yer heid? Yer goin' doaty? Yer know who this belongs tae? It's ony Mike McGovern's and he's put the word out...If yer found wi' this on yer wrist, yer'll 'ave nae fingers to fasten the strap. Get it out o' my shop with it, noo!'

Stewart shoved it back in his pocket and headed for the door. Jimmy turned back to ask: 'Is it real, Mister Grier?'

'Ay, it's bloody real, yer doaty bampot!'

Mike McGovern, the second crime-lord in the town, hard as nails and with three strapping sons.

Stewart and Jimmy were sitting back round the kitchen table. 'So, tell me again, Jimmy. You were walking down the street with the sausage rolls...'

'I was walking down the street and this man...'

'So what was the man like, Jimmy? Could it 'a been Mike McGovern, Jimmy?'

'I could ony see 'im from the back, but he got into Mike's Daimler.'

'And why didnae yer mention this, Jimmy?'

'Yer didnae ask, Stewie.'

'Jeeeeeeeeez...'

Stewart, not for the first time, put his head in his hands and wondered how long his boss would expect this 'shaping up' of his son and heir to last.

'Dinnae get crabbit wi' me, Stewie.'

Stewart gave up. Nearly. 'Come on, laddie, let's go to Turrie's Caff an get a wee bite to eat. We've decisions to make.'

Turrie's Caff was hot and steamy inside, the place full of yabbering youths. They managed to find an empty table and when Ellie, the waitress, came over they ordered four black pudding rolls. 'Kin I have a wee sausage on mine, as well?' asked Jimmy, hopefully. She had a soft spot for Jimmy.

'Course you can, you great lummox,' she said and went off to get the food.

'Brenda told me something last night,' Jimmy said when they were alone. 'Aboot ma da.'

'What?'

'Well, yer know how ma da told us he'd got rid of his fingerprints with a blowtorch a wee while back?'

'Yeah.'

'Well, Brenda said he'd done it by accident, taking a Mars bar out of the chip pan.'

Stewart's response was spared by a sudden draught from the open door as five or six members of the McGovern gang barged through and went straight over to the pool table. The couple who had been quietly enjoying a friendly game put their cues down and melted away to a table in the corner.

'Oh, no, I cannae believe it,' said Stewart.

'Have they come a-lookin' for the watch?' whispered Jimmy, a bit too loudly. There was fear in his eyes.

'Nae, but dinnae say aught.'

But Jimmy had already caught the eye of Tommy Rankin, five foot three and the physique of an undernourished whippet, but probably the meanest most vicious guy in Arbermouth. Jimmy sat like a rabbit caught in the headlights as Tommy fixed him with a snarl. 'What youse lookin' at?'

'Nothin', Tammy, nothin'. Jimmy stammered. He couldn't have

looked more guilty if he'd tried. 'We don't know nuthin' about…nuthin' do we Stewie?'

Tommy pointed the cue at him and Stewart could feel a broken head coming on.

'Yer off yer heid, man, yer talkin' mince!' said Tommy, turning away in disgust.

'Cut that oot, Tammy,' Stewart chipped in, 'an skedaddle aff.'

'What you say, mon? Oh, it's wee Stewie, Shiela's mon. We all know Shiela, eh lads?' The group behind him were all sniggering now and making rude gestures. 'Yeah, Shiela Mc-bloody-Dougall; I wouldnae ride 'er in tae battle, she's a face like a bulldog lickin' piss off a nettle!'

'Dinnae you…' Stewart was stopped as he jumped up by a very firm hand on his shoulder: Michael McGurk. Six foot six of pure muscle and feared by everybody in the town, from both sides of the fence.

'Now, now, children; calm doon, play nice. Dinnae get yerselves into a right fankle. Mr McG wouldnae like it, nither would Mr McD.' There was silence in Turrie's caff as everyone held their breath. 'Now, you two, gang awa' an' go bile yer heids.' Stewart dragged Jimmy out and back to the car.

'I cannae trust you to keep your nashgab closed kinnae? Yer greet numpty.'

Jimmy hung his head. ''S no fair, I didnae finish ma sausage.'

'Look, Jimmy, let's get home, I have a cunning plan.'

'Right! We have to get rid of this wee watch, soon as we can, Jimmy. McGovern will murdurr us; if we're lucky. There'll be war if yer da finds out. We have to take the Rolex down to London, sell it there.'

'Kin I no keep it, Stew…Stewart?'

'No.'

'Kin I have a wee peep then?' Stewart took out the Rolex and put it on the table.

'Now, look, dinnae touch, then leave it there and go get the Toyota out the garage. We'll have to fill her up on the way doon.'

Jimmy wasn't driving yet, well, not legally, but he liked to manoeuvre the huge Toyota Land Cruiser in and out of the garage. It was his father's car really, but given to Stewart for 'company business'. Jimmy looked down at the Rolex on his wrist, he hadn't been able to resist slipping it on. He loved the shiny green face surrounded by *white* gold. He loved the fact that it told him it was Thursday, because sometimes he forgot what day it was. He struggled with the Toyota's fancy locking system, tugging at the driver's door before it was properly unlocked. Eventually it opened and he slipped into the driver's seat. He looked at the enormous panel of shiny controls, and he was in charge! He was so excited, it was like sitting at the controls of an Airbus A340, like the model in his bedroom. The Toyota started with a purr like a tiger. Off to London! What an adventure! And Stewart had promised to buy him a watch with a green face all of his own when he got the thirty thousand pounds. He put the car into reverse and slowly backed out.

Pity they hadn't had time to get the clasp mended.

Pity Jimmy hadn't noticed when the Rolex slid from his wrist onto the garage floor just behind the front wheel.

Pity he didn't hear the crunch as the Rolex was squashed as flat as a wee pancake.

Qi Transfer

COLIN BALMER

The Victorian mansion should not have been a gloomy residence for Florence on her fifth wedding anniversary. She had inherited the family home when her widowed mother, Alice, passed away six years ago at the beginning of the twentieth century and had gladly accepted the marriage proposal from coal merchant Herbert Braggins. But life had not been so exciting for the young bride lately as a debilitating illness had her confined to bed for a large part of each day and these long, lonely nights.

Florence is in that ephemeral state between fluid sleep and solid waking. She looks through a grey wispy haze, trying to identify the spectral shape that slowly materialises. The shadowy mist parts and the haggard, wrinkled pale face of her mother emerges.

"Mama, what are you doing here?" she asks.

Grey, emotionless eyes, reinforce the coldness of her reply, "I come to warn you. That man is not good for you."

"What?"

The vision disappears slowly with no further words as the frail young woman opens her eyes wide and reassures herself, "It's only a dream."

Now wide awake, she squints through the dawn twilight, reaches to lift a candlestick from the walnut inlaid whatnot. Last night's ashes throw no heat from the grate into the winter bedroom. With trembling fingers, she lights the candle. In the flickering light, she lifts on a heavy velvet dressing robe and shuffles out of the bedroom. She is frustrated by the lethargic pace that contradicts her age. With no offspring she cannot blame serial pregnancies, like her contemporaries, for her ungainly gait.

Her husband has heard her movement and meets her at the top of the stairs.

"Now don't you be exerting yourself, my dear. Get back in bed and I'll bring you some breakfast and your medicine and light the fire, you look cold."

She forces a weak smile. "You're my angel, Herbert. I don't know where I'd be without you. When I get better, we'll do the tour around Europe together."

She returns to the comfort of the mahogany four poster and lays her head on the tower of duck down pillows. He returns with a light breakfast of scrambled egg. She turns down his offer to spoon feed her but accepts the dose of unpleasant liquid he pours from a green bottle.

"Take this, it will help you get better."

"Arggh! It's horrible, but you know best. I'll have to get used to it, won't I?"

"Yes, and you know it helps you relax and makes you more comfortable."

She is not now bothered by the dream and does not tell him of Alice. True to the promise of the medicine, she has a warm feeling of optimism. After an hour in bed, she feels light-headed, and a stroll seems a good idea. She follows the oak-panelled corridor to the library where she settles before the escritoire to continue the diary she started after her marriage. When her appetite told her it was lunch time, she went slowly downstairs for a light snack of game pie. After this exertion, she retired to bed for the rest of the afternoon until dinner. Her husband had added the coals and put in the warming pan to prepare her bed. At night-time Herbert brought dinner on a tray to her in bed. A glass of Bordeaux helped to quash the taste of the evening dose of medicine. And she drifted off to a contented sleep.

The following morning, the dream reappears, but the visit lasts longer, the vision clearer and her mother more insistent.

"You must get away from that awful man. He wants everything that I left to you."

"But Mama, I love him, and he loves me. See how he cares for me! You know that my property became his when we got married, so he has it already."

Her mother protests again and then her ghostly figure fades away.

The day passes in a comparable way to before, with a short walk to the library to write her diary, although Florence does not have the strength to descend two flights of stone stairs for have lunch downstairs. She takes all meals and treatment in her room.

As the week progresses, her energy evaporates to the extent that she cannot reach the library and, so, spends all day in her room, where her only amusement is writing her diary. But consoled, fed and medicated by doting Herbert.

As her strength fades, her mother's attendance becomes longer, more physical than spectral and much more demanding.

"I left you this big house and the estate, which is his by marriage as you say. But he still wants to be rid of you even if it seems he's trying to nurse you back to health. Somehow, I feel more alive as you seem to be fading. I can't understand it, but please listen to me."

Alice hasn't the awareness of mystic eastern philosophy, or she might recognise the *qi* of Chinese culture. This vital life force is considered to be in all of us and unites life, body and spirit. The experience of the deceased mother and dying child enabled, somehow, a qi transmission between the two. And so it is that the elder woman can now directly participate in the material world.

Now Florence is bedridden all day, her husband introduces youthful Stephanie to help with his nursing. Together they provide for all her physical and medical needs without showing their anticipation of her imminent departure from this life.

On the morning of the month's anniversary of her initial confinement, Florence can barely open her eyes for her mother's visit, but experiences, nevertheless, a fuller cerebral dialogue with Alice.

"Florence, now I can see the full picture. Your nurse, Stephanie, is more commonly known as the Gaiety Theatre actress Fanny Brewer. Your husband has been in a relationship with her for the last two months. The medicine that they are dosing you with is a cocktail of rat poison and laudanum, which is the drug that gives you the euphoric lift. You aren't physically capable of doing anything other than refusing the poison, but I suspect they will force it down your throat if necessary. I will have to get involved and talk to Herbert or frighten that little tramp. I can hear him on the stairs now – so no time like the present!"

Florence drifts into a coma. Alice slips out of the door to confront the would-be killer.

Herbert stops in his tracks on the top step of the staircase.

"What? Who? How?...

Precariously balanced, he tumbles backwards with a very little push.

Two weeks after her mother had resolved the conflict, Florence has returned to full health after stopping the medication. The nurse has not shown up since. No longer sustained by her daughter's qi, Alice the spectre no longer appears. A fresh-faced young lady-of-means, one of

Belgravia's more attractive widows attends the Coroners' Court. The coroner's report concludes that Herbert had smashed his head and died instantly when falling down the stone staircase. The report speculated that he may have been under the influence of laudanum. He was well-known as a frequent client of the local apothecary.

Synergy

Air and water
bricks and mortar

Belt and braces
shoes and laces

Canoe and paddle
stirrups and saddle

Drain and gutter
bread and butter

Egg and spoon
sun and moon

Fence and gate
roof and slate

Grape and vine
cheese and wine

Hip and thigh
collar and tie

Iron and steel
rod and reel

Judge and jury
lib'dem and tory

Kiss and cuddle
pool and puddle

Ladder and rungs
liver and lungs

Mast and sail
stumps and bail

Nut and bolt
crypt and vault

Orb and sceptre
pollen and nectar

Plug and socket
chain and locket

Queen and castle
church and chapel

Rock and roll
flag and pole

Sword and shield
signed and sealed

Tyre and tread
needle and thread

U and me
pod and pea

Verb and noun
jewel and crown

Wave and ripple
breast and nipple

X and y
live and die

Yoko and lennon
mortise and tenon

Zig and zag
cliff and crag

WARREN DAVIES

Travelling Light

DAVID LOCKLEY

'Damn,' I thought as my eyes snapped open in the darkness, 'Wide awake again.'

I have been a martyr to insomnia for as long as I can remember. I have tried everything. Herbal teas, breathing exercises, counting sheep. A friend of mine even suggested buying a new mattress. I told him I'd sleep on it, ha ha. No, he didn't laugh either.

I lay still for a few minutes, hoping to drop off again but knowing that the Sandman had well and truly buggered off for the rest of that night.

Surrendering myself to the inevitable, I sat up in my dishevelled single bed and switched on my bedside lamp. I made it a point to never look at the time on these occasions. If I knew what time it was, then I would also know how much time there was left to elapse before my alarm went off. And nothing is more likely to keep me awake than counting off those sleepless minutes and hours as the alarm bell approaches with the inevitability of death.

Instead, I reached for the notebook and pen that I keep beside my bed. I sometimes find that writing a to-do list for the following day helps to calm my mind, transferring tasks and worries from brain to paper. However, on that night, for some unexplained reason, a different imperative gripped me.

I placed the nib of the cheap Bic on the paper and, after a few seconds of introspection, I started to scribble, while memories puffed up like a plume of sediment from the bottom of a dark pond.

> *'When I was at school,'* I wrote, *'there was a girl called Joanne. I mentioned to my friend Ian that I thought she had a fish-face. I would never have said that to Joanne herself, of course. But Ian, with the kind of blind insensitivity that only kids display, went to Joanne and told her what I had said about her. I can't imagine how that must have made her feel. It was made worse by the fact that someone told me later that Joanne had been fond of me. Anyway, Joanne, wherever you are now, (hopefully married and settled and happy) I am truly sorry. Signed, Kevin.'*

Detaching it from the notepad, I stared at the piece of paper and wondered why I had been compelled to write that down, after all these years. And I also wondered what I should do with it now. I fumbled in the top drawer of my bedside cabinet, studiously avoiding the digital display of my alarm clock, and produced a lighter. I have never smoked but I have sometimes lit incense cones in the bedroom as yet another potential insomnia cure. Hence the lighter.

I flicked it till a tiny flame added its light to the gentle glow from my lamp. I then introduced flame to paper and then had a moment of panic as the scribbled note caught and burned. I waved it frantically in the air until the flames went out (mercifully before reaching my fingers). 'Well,' I thought, 'that was stupid'. Most of the note had been reduced to ash and black flakes which were now scattered on my bedclothes. As the little cloud of smoke spread itself around, I wondered how close I had come to setting the bed, the room, the house and myself on fire.

However, I did feel that the uncomfortable memory of that childhood indiscretion suddenly seemed lessened somehow. Still there but diffuse and insubstantial.

After a few moments, I picked up the pen and started writing on the next page of my notepad.

> *'When I got my first job in a shop, I told my colleague Phil what the alarm code was to open up the following morning, (I was on a late shift). However, it turned out that I had told him the wrong code and, inevitably, the alarm went off, causing all kinds of security shenanigans and getting Phil into trouble. I swore blind that I had given him the correct code and that the fault was entirely his. But I secretly knew that I had inadvertently given the wrong code. I never owned up. Anyway, if you're out there, Phil, (hopefully a captain of industry or managing director or something by now), I'm truly sorry. Signed, Kevin.'*

I stared at the piece of paper and quickly decided that my previous experiment with the lighter was, at best, ill-judged. This time I ripped the paper into tiny fragments which I shuffled together into my hand. Clambering out of bed, I headed to the bathroom where I dropped the fragments into the toilet bowl, like a tiny, very unmagical snowfall. I pulled the flush and watched the fragments swirl around and disappear. Unfortunately, when the flush had ended and the waters had stilled, there were still a few pieces of paper floating around. I knew another flush would probably sort that out but their persistence disturbed me. It was as if they were hanging around in a sort of accusatory manner. I also wondered about the kinds of paper you could flush down a toilet and the kinds that might cause a blockage.

Still, I had to admit that my thoughts of Phil and the alarm now felt strangely abstract. Turning off the bathroom light I headed back to bed.

My next note outlined the time I got hopelessly drunk one night and threw up in the back of a taxi even though I had assured the taxi driver upon entering the cab that I wouldn't, ('*anyway, Mr Taxi Driver, I am very sorry, signed, Kevin*'). I folded that one into a paper plane, went over to my bedroom window, which was already open on that mild summer night, and sent it soaring out into the neighbourhood. However, my abhorrence of litter suddenly pained my conscience and I wondered in whose garden my nocturnal confession would land.

I took my next note, ('*...anyway, Mother, I am very sorry, signed Kevin*') to the kitchen and, having screwed it into a ball, I dropped it into the compost bin. 'There', I thought, 'instant absolution'. However, the compost bin was already quite full and I didn't think I could fit another confession in there to nestle amongst the tea bags and carrot peel.

I still had a few troubling memories to scribble down but I was starting to run out of means of disposal. But, after making use of the food blender, the toaster and a bottle of bleach, I eventually came to my final note.

> '*When I first started going out with Rachel, I also fancied her mate Kimberley. When it became apparent that Kimberley quite liked me too, I went on a few dates with her, behind Rachel's back, claiming 'nights out with the lads' as an excuse. Although nothing came of it (although not from want of trying) I never confessed to Rachel and she doesn't know about my infidelity to this day. Anyway, Rachel, I am very sorry. Signed, Kevin*'.

I looked at this note for a long time before putting on a pair of slippers, opening my back door and shuffling out into the dark of my back garden. It's not a big garden but I have a couple of flowerbeds on either side. Kneeling on the chilly ground, I used my fingers to excavate a tiny grave in the soil and, with feelings of solemnity and ceremony, I placed this last note into the hollow and covered it over, patting the soil down with my hand.

It was at that moment that I became aware of a glow turning the night a dark grey, then sepia, then gold as the morning sun slowly made its appearance and illuminated the garden with an almost heavenly light.

Getting to my feet and brushing dirt and blades of grass from my hands and the knees of my pyjama trousers, I made my way back indoors and into my bedroom. The shafts of sunlight fell upon the morning suit that hung from the door handle of my wardrobe.

I hadn't had much sleep but I still felt ready and able to embrace the big day ahead. The day that Rachel and I would walk up the aisle and start our new lives together as man and wife.

And now I felt, as we started on that journey together, that I would be travelling much lighter than I might have done otherwise.

A smile came to my lips as my alarm clock started to beep.

Too Cold to Sing

There they stood at the village cross,
Two nights before Christmas and all was still,
The frost on the grass had been there all day,
And the moon was rising above the hill.

The band assembled, instruments glinting
In the feeble glow of the only streetlight,
In their coats and scarves and fingerless gloves
They were tuned up and ready to play Silent Night.

As the choir stood around, all clearing their throats,
The choir master waited to make the air ring
With the beautiful sounds of the carols they'd learned,
But no sounds came out, it was too cold to sing.

BARBARA SHEARWOOD

Dead Wood

PAUL MULDOON

The coffin slipped through the velvet curtains into oblivion. Tommy had seen and heard enough so he quietly exited the crematorium by the back door. His order book was full and he needed to get back to the workshop. He was thrilled that the idea had at last come to fruition; things had moved along fast since his appearance on television.

It was a far cry from his first creations: a bird table to keep the cat at arm's length from his feathered friends. Garden planters for his wife, Anne, to fill with summer bedding plants. Family and friends took notice and Tommy was always happy enough to knock something up for them at a minimal cost. He couldn't charge for the material as it was all recycled – he had the job of ripping it out of the buildings he was working on as a joiner, buildings that were being refurbished. It was a crime in Tommy's eyes; oak, beech, even teak and occasionally mahogany, all destined for the skip, only to be replaced by the far inferior laminated chipboard, MDF or worse still, plastic!

So he took it upon himself to rescue this unwanted treasure the earth had given to his predecessors, take it home and give it a new life. He started small but had the help of his wife, a frustrated design student who had successfully completed an art and design diploma at college, only to find no work available for her in that field and ended up in the typing pool at a local insurance company. So when Tommy's creations and workshop grew over the years, she would add her artistic touch to each piece to make it unique. The garden benches and conservatory tables were snatched up quickly, stools and benches all made their appearance in the workshop, a nice little earner for the family purse, especially when e-Bay came along and strangers were bidding for his efforts. He made far more than he had been charging family and friends.

His conversations with many of the buyers were nearly always centred round the fact that his products were created from recycled timber. They were happy that, in their eyes, use was being made of a precious commodity – no tree was being felled for their bench or bed frame. They were surprised that some of the oak had indeed come from the railway sleepers Tommy could pick up for a song at local reclamation yards.

Once the ugly veneer had been removed with the help of his band saw, underneath was a perfectly acceptable, beautifully grained piece of nature that was a sight for sore eyes, especially when given a coat of varnish.

Then, out of the blue, six months ago, tragedy struck the family. Anne's father, Barry, died very suddenly from a massive heart attack and it was left up to Anne and Tommy to make most of the funeral arrangements. It was at this sad time for the family that some of life's reality hit home to Tommy, dying was an expensive business! He perused all the costs and was inevitably drawn to the high cost of the coffin. Why was it so costly? After all, in many cases it was destined to the fires of the crematorium. Why, he asked himself, could the cost not be kept lower with the use of recycled timber? Why not try it for yourself? thought Tommy.

So, after a couple of months of mourning, he put his idea to Anne that he might try this new venture and see if the market was ready. After all, his feedback from his furniture clients was always positive about the use of recycling, why not for coffins? He put together a few designs with Anne's input, a coat of varnish and, Hey Presto! It looked the part, but the local funeral directors were not too impressed; second-hand timber would not go down well with their clients, he was told, even though the designs were acceptable.

He didn't believe them. He knew there were enough eco warriors and avid recyclers out there that would be interested. 'Why not try Dragon's Den on the telly?' Anne suggested. And why not? thought Tommy.

The product was quirky enough to interest the producers, so they gave Tommy his five minutes of fame one Sunday night. He only wanted publicity, so he asked a high price for a low equity, and sure enough, one by one of the Dragons announced: 'I'm out!' 'I'm out!' 'I'm out!' You might be out tonight, thought Tommy, but one day you'll all be 'In!' – if not mine, then someone else's coffin.

So he left the Den with no extra funds but it seems an awful lot of publicity, and enquiries started to come into the funeral directors who had been so negative towards him, and soon enough he had his first firm order. Barry's widow had been in touch with the funeral directors she had appointed and instructed them to use one of Tommy's recycled timber coffins. She had even been able to get in touch with Tommy to discuss ideas and was well pleased with 'BARRY R.I.P' etched onto the sides of the coffin. Barry, it turns out, was indeed an eco-warrior and 'friend of the earth' as his widow put it and cutting down a tree to use for his cremation was against all he had stood for. So she was more than happy with Tommy's idea, and, yes, as it was his first firm order, he was welcome to attend the service down at Agecroft Crematorium. He mingled with the mourners long enough to hear their comments:

'It's made by that bloke that was on Dragon's Den!'

'It's very smart!'

'I like the etching on the side of the coffin.'

All the comments were positive and it was rubber-stamped by the fact that since Barry's order, seven more coffins had been requested, so, as Tommy made his way back to his car, past the many rows of headstones, he was thinking: 'There's certainly a lot of money to be made from dying,' and, stretching out his arm, said to himself: 'Today Agecroft, tomorrow the underworld!'

Edukashun

VERONICA SCOTTON

In 1956, on my first day of school, I remember hiding behind my mam while she spoke to the teacher in front of the class. Therefore, I can only suspect that I didn't join the school with the rest of the class at the beginning of September.

However, what I do remember was that we had respect for the teacher. Or did we just respect the fact that he or she was allowed, perhaps expected, to bully, humiliate, and abuse their pupils. They could hit you with a cane especially made for the purpose, or if that wasn't handy, a ruler would do. This could be handed out for talking in class, defacing school furniture, insubordination or even not learning the timetables that had been set for homework. If the class teacher was disinclined to use their own energy, they could send you to the Head. This prolonged the agony as you often had to wait outside, in the corridor until he got round to it, where everyone passing could pass judgement in word or deed.

The pupils at St John's RC Girls School, where I attended were, I presume, all from working class homes, but within this class there were subtle sub classes, and you definitely knew the pecking order.

There were the ones that had to share a bed and would sometimes come to school smelling of wee, when their younger sibling had wet the bed. The end of a towel or rag, dipped under a cold tap, might be sufficient to wash your hands and neck, but a bath was needed to rid you of the smell of urine and who could afford, or have time, to put a shilling in the meter, turn on the immersion heater, bring in the tin bath from the yard and soak, especially mid-week.

Fortunately, our family was not that low. Our mam made sure we were all out of nappy's months before we were two years old. She needed them for the next baby on the way. And, we all had a bed each. In hindsight I am astonished at the amount of work she got through, because she made the beds every day and stripped, washed, and ironed the bedding every week, no mean feat with nine beds. We also always had clean clothes to wear due to her weekly trip to the wash house, which I realise now was a bit of me-time, while slaving over an industrial washing machine, dryer, and ironing board, she was drinking tea and gossiping with her friends.

There was another class, perhaps the majority that smelled of nicotine, since in those days cigarettes apparently were good for your health and film stars glamorized the habit. Living in very small back-to-back houses there was no escape from the fog created by two adult chain smokers. I didn't realize that I was among these smelly children until I got a Saturday job, packing bags behind the tills in a supermarket, and was taken aside by a supervisor who very furtively asked how often I washed my hair. Embarrassment is too weak a word to describe how I felt. My mother looked askance at me when I suddenly started bathing more often, and especially washing my hair, didn't I realise that I was washing all the strength out of it? Some good came out of my embarrassment however as she then started bathing my younger siblings more often. Unfortunately for her however, this resulted in making more work for her, which she would remind us of with a martyr's sigh, as she washed the scum ring from around the bath. Also, I presume that the lack of personal hygiene served me well as I now have a very high level of antibodies and rarely get sick.

Above these two classes were the kids that came into school wearing more upmarket clothing, machine made cardigans from C & A or Marks and Spencer and clothes that fit properly, not bought to grow into. I remember one girl, who had beautiful curly hair, cut at the hairdressers, telling her clique with horror that while sharing a bath with her little sister, the sister had "done her biz in the bath." From a distance I listened to the dramatic replies. From where I stood, I thought "Wow she has a bath in her house."

I remember that there were some teachers who managed to instil knowledge into our brains without resorting to violence, and some that even brought joy to our days, but I very much doubt that they would allow the behaviour of today's children. Nowadays children learn their rights, in the way we learned the catechism or timetables, but not balanced with a list of responsibilities.

During my childhood, if they had problems at home, children would shamefully hide it. Perhaps out of necessity whisper the problem to the teacher who would allow them to stay in at break or have the morning off. Nowadays pupils shout out to the whole world with pride, that they have a social worker, their father is in prison, they've got anxiety issues. They are excused when they kick a teacher in the shins because "poor little lamb, his parents won't buy him an upgrade for his Play Station, and this has caused inferiority issues amongst his friends."

The thing that has got me reminiscing in this way is my recent experience of adult learning. I'm astonished that people who have, I presume, spent more than 10 years in education in the UK still don't have the ability to sit quietly in class, show little respect for the teacher and will stroll in class half an hour late with not even an excuse or apology, let alone a note from a parent.

I was brought up by a strict mother and an obedient father, to have unbending morals: don't swear, steal, tell lies, answer back and up to a point I think I passed this on to my own kids (though I swore that I would be a different kind of mother than mine). Strict codes of black and white, good, and bad. Children were expected to behave, be seen, and not heard, obedient without question.

Five weeks ago, on my first day in the classroom, I was shocked and dismayed at the behaviour of these childish adults, but my opinion has taken a subtle change. The badly behaved pupils are entertaining, the time flies. When someone interrupts the teacher in mid-sentence, it is often to ask a question, that it had not occurred to me to ask. The teacher in turn, has no stick to beat us with and so must use different tactics to get the subject across. He has infinite patience and respect for everyone and my opinion of him (my first assumption that he was a scruffy, lazy individual) has gone up a notch.

The learners, misfits that have somehow slipped through the education net, are gradually becoming less anxious, more confident, and ever more joyful at each triumph.

And in their own way becoming more respectful to the teacher.

The Primrose Path

DAVID LOCKLEY

The avenue was made up of modest terraced houses, cosy and anonymous, nestling shoulder to shoulder and presenting the impassive faces of their facades in a neat line. But there, in the middle of the row, was a space, like a toothless gap in an otherwise benign smile. A patch of scruffy grass, more grey than green in the streetlight, where, presumably, a house had once stood.

She walked home alone from her evening shift at the shop several times a week. Her parents were frantic with worry about her wandering the streets at night but neither of them drove to pick her up and, anyway, she assured them that she rarely saw another soul on her way home.

And every time she walked along this avenue, she found herself wondering about that jarring space in the middle of the row of houses. And the aspect of it that fascinated her the most was the garden path that still cut through the grass like a long-healed scar. The path that just stopped at the point where a long-forgotten door would once have stood.

She always walked quite briskly, eager to reach the safety and comfort of her own home. But she often found herself slowing her pace as she went past the strange space, with its looming atmosphere of unsettling absence. That little patch of void with the gravelled intrusion of that obsolete path. Sometimes she stopped altogether and just stared in a silent reverie, before shaking herself back to reality and hurrying home.

But not tonight. Tonight, she paused even longer than usual as she stared at the grass and the path. For there, fringing both edges of the path along its six-metre length, was a row of primroses, the yellow of their petals still bright and joyous, even in the shadows of the night.

Had they been there before? she wondered. How could she not have noticed them the last time she walked past this spot? How fast do primroses grow?

All these questions drifted through her mind as she watched the tiny, flamboyant heads of the flowers dance in the night breezes.

She didn't know what made her take the first step. Maybe it was the silent welcome that the flowers implied, but after a few moments of hesitation, she started to walk along the path. After a few steps, she came to its end, seeing only grass around her in the general size and shape of a house. But then, she took one more step.

She gasped as the space around her changed. The fresh, open-air smell of the Spring night seemed to vanish to be replaced by a musty, indoor fug. The houses of the avenue, faintly illuminated by the antiseptic glare of the streetlight, became faint as the sight of grimy walls seemed to solidify around her, like a gradually thickening bank of fog.

She could start to perceive details, a grimy pattern on peeling wallpaper, damp patches on mottled plaster, dark, ancient woodwork. With each second, the grim interior of a shabby house coalesced around her. She took a few steps forward, her fascination momentarily overtaking her foreboding. But then, a nameless dread made her skin crawl and the blood freeze in her veins.

She turned around to flee back down the path but, instead of the moonlit street she was expecting to see, she was confronted by the pitted wood of a door, solid and impassable. A sound behind her made her turn back to the awful house where a dark looming shape rushed towards her, grasping hands outstretched towards her throat. She took a deep breath to scream but the scream never came.

It had been about a week since the woman had disappeared, mused the little girl as she looked out of her bedroom window to the moonlit street below. The police had knocked on the door of every house along the route the woman was known to take on her walk home from work. However, nobody had seen her and nobody could explain her disappearance.

It was all very dramatic and a bit exciting, thought the little girl as she gazed at the patch of grass across the road from her house. The sight of that empty space with the garden path still there, leading to nowhere, always gave her a little morbid thrill. Her friends at school had once told her that there used to be a house there but it was demolished years ago when it was discovered that the man who had lived there was a monster, luring young women into the terrible confines of his lair and brutally murdering them. They said that the police had found body parts and pieces of preserved skin all over the house. Nobody could bear to think of such an evil house existing so the bulldozers had moved in. At least, that's what she had been told.

But she couldn't believe such nonsense. Especially not as the pretty, yellow speckling of a row of primroses now lined the strange little path. Their tiny heads bobbed and weaved and seemed to call to her to tiptoe downstairs, slip out of her front door, cross the quiet street and dance along the length of the path.

She watched the flowers for a while before letting her curtain fall closed, turning and walking towards her bedroom door.

Space Lamb

Mary had a little lamb and this is what she thought
I'll train this clever little lamb to be an astronaut
She found she didn't need to, for this lamb was very smart
It was aero-dynamic, all it had to do was fart
Now this was very useful as Mary soon found out
The wind came in quite handy, of this there was no doubt.
It didn't take much fuelling, quite cheap to run, it seems
All that it required was unending tins of beans
The local supermarket was her source of supply
The code-word for her project was, 'reaching for the sky'
The manager was very sympathetic to her plight
He couldn't wait to see if Mary's little lamb took flight
The lamb was quite oblivious and thought "what's all the fuss?"
But then perhaps a lamb just wouldn't think the same as us
As Mary schemed and plotted, the lamb was quite content
To fart into the bottles that Mary sold as scent.
At least that's what she told him, but something wasn't right
And so the little lamb stole into Mary's lab that night
"It's not what I expected." He pondered, in surprise
He read the secret plans and he could not believe his eyes.
"It might be quite exciting to take off in the blue.
Visit another planet. Yes! That's what I'd like to do"
And so the little lamb began to make plans of his own
He didn't like the thought much, of living all alone
He searched through 'perfect partners' to see if he could find
A pretty girl who wouldn't mind leaving the earth behind.

At last he found the travelling companion of his dreams

It seems he's not the only one who's rather fond of beans

With bated breath he made arrangements for them both to meet

At the local supermarket at the bottom of the street

She was everything he'd hoped for. They didn't want to part.

They married. Soon they had a child.

A proper little fart.

Now Mary was excited about her stroke of luck

Soon they were on their way to cape Canaveral in a truck

A military escort showed them around the place.

He asked the lamb "how do you feel 'bout zooming into space?"

"I'm looking forward to it." Was the little lamb's reply.

"I can't wait to find out just what lies beyond the sky.

Maybe I'll find a planet that no one found before.

For all I know it might turn out to be a proper bore.

Maybe I'll find a planet with a great expanse of green.

Maybe there will be a lot of nothing to be seen."

Then as he spoke, a look of wonder flashed across his face.

With that he gave a great big fart and zoomed off into space

MARY YOUNG

The Red Leather Journal

VERONICA SCOTTON

Suzy picked up the journal and brought it to her nose. It still evoked the memory of that Christmas, years past when she had received it from her grandfather. Not only the smell of the leather, but also her memory of him, the slightly wiffy, grandad. He hadn't washed often after her Nanna had passed away, his threadbare jumper smelled of the manure of his garden, his breath of cigarettes, his house slightly musty and damp. He had never got rid of her belongings, her clothes were still hanging in the wardrobe, her Chanel No5 on the dresser, her hairbrush still with silver hair in the bristles.

To his granddaughter, the stale smell clinging to her grandad, was the smell of calm, away from the frosty atmosphere of her parents' disintegrating marriage. He didn't go in for cuddles and kissing and whenever she let herself into the forever unlocked door to his house, he would comment, "What! are you here again?" He would put a kettle on and make her a cup of very sweet, milky tea and put it down on the kitchen table. Her mother would object strongly if she knew, sugar was banned in Suzy's diet, it was bad for her teeth and skin - her mother thought it was bad for her weight too but never voiced that opinion, it wasn't politicly correct or kind to mention to a child that she was getting a bit thick round the waist.

Suzie would get out her homework from school and work on it in companiable silence, while Grandad whittled away at the ship he was creating in a bottle, or the doll's house which was intended for her, but for which he continued to find improvements. Once the homework was completed, he would join her at the kitchen table and together they would play their favourite game. With closed eyes they would each use a pencil to touch a word in the paper and write it down. Using the random words, they would compete to compose the most outlandish stories. At the time Suzy did not appreciate that these games were lessons to increase her vocabulary and set her up for the famous author she was to become.

On Suzy's 13th birthday, her first thought was of excitement for the day ahead, her mum had promised her a "girlie day" having a trip to the hairdresser and manicurist. The first time ever, usually her mum trimmed her hair, there wasn't much money to spare in the Morrison household. Suddenly a loud crash and the sound of her parents screaming at each other broke the reverie, she hid her head under the blankets to block out the hateful words pouring from her father's mouth and the self-righteousness retorts from her mother.

The door slammed and silence reigned for a while. She crept down the stairs to find her father sitting alone in stony silence staring into space. Her birthday was forgotten.

Over the next few weeks Suzy discovered the reason for the culmination of her parents' marriage, when her mum came to take her out for a belated birthday treat and then to the very upmarket one bed flat in the heart of the city. When she had realized that her missed periods were not caused by the stress of keeping a marriage and an affair afloat, it was too late for an abortion. Her married lover was happy to set her up in a flat, better for him that she was where he could drop in and see her when it suited. But accommodating a teenage daughter, was out of the question. At home, Suzy felt embarrassment with her father's "bit on the side", although she suspected it was her father's tit for tat retaliation, rather than an overwhelming love affair. It made sense that she moves in with grandad.

It suited Suzy, his house was closer to the High School she attended, she gradually took over the housework and her grandad became slightly less nose blind. Often her dad would drop by to see her, loath to admit how lonely he had become, boasting of new contracts and promotions or about team building outings. Suzy suspected he was hoping to impress his dad, but grandad rarely showed his approval. One evening he dropped in on the way home from work and noticed her dinner plate pushed to the side as she played the game her grandad had invented, the stories now getting more and more outrageous as her vocabulary expanded. Her dad remarked about the discarded food, and she answered casually, "It's OK dad, grandad can warm it up in the microwave for his lunch tomorrow!"

She was shocked when her dad's fist came down hard on the table and he let out a roar, then stormed out of the house.

Grandad was very quiet, his head bowed, Suzy was confused. "What was that all about?" she asked.

He sighed and answered. 'Suzy don't be mad with your dad, it's my fault. When he was born, there was no instructions on how to bring up children. I was working all hours to earn enough money for a deposit for this house and the census in those days was 'spare the rod, spoil the child' I always insisted that he eat everything on his plate no matter how

54

long he had to sit there. One day your nanna and I, noticed a rancid smell coming from the dining room and followed our noses to the drawer in the table, where we found all the food that he had been unable to stomach. I put him over my knee and smacked him. He never left food again."

Suzy could not imagine her grandad losing his temper in that way and went to bed where she cried for the sad little boy who had grown into her dad. The story was never mentioned again, but she became more tolerant and understanding of her taciturn father.

She was sixteen, waiting for GCSE results and looking forward to college when she came home to notice her dad's car outside grandad's house and hearing raised voices.

"You are the most selfish man, you never change, what do you think this will do to Suzy, she adores you."

Suzy stopped in her tracks and listened unapologetically as her grandad answered sadly, "Yes I know, but you will never know how much I have missed Lily since she passed, I didn't want to delay the time when we could be together."

Her dad's answer came back scornfully, "What utter rot! Afterlife? You don't really believe in all that rubbish?"

He came barging out of the door almost bowling Suzy over. He hugged her and began to cry, then without a word climbed into his car and drove away.

It took her a while to prise the answers to her questions from her grandad and sobbed uncontrollably as he admitted ignoring the signs of bowel cancer for several years and that now the only treatment open to him was palliative care, he had a couple of months to live at the most.

It was easy to forget that he was ill, they still picked up random words and made stories, they still sat in his garden and predicted which flowers would be popping up once again in spring. As the days turned cooler, they talked about Christmas coming. Suzy now had a half-brother and relationships had thawed between her parents to the point where she could bring him to visit grandad. He would cuddle the little boy in a way that he had never done with her or her dad. He would stroke his blond hair and sigh, perhaps regretting the closeness that he had never shared with his own son.

By December he had lost a lot of weight, he'd lost his appetite and was sleeping half the day. On his good days he would wrap up warm and venture out, walking as far as his strength would allow, filing to memory the beauty of the world that he would soon leave behind. One evening he handed Suzy a present wrapped in Christmas wrapping and told her to open it.

"I want to watch you open it before I go."

Choking back tears she opened the heavy red journal, and the smell caressed her senses.

He spoke softly to her, "I know you are going to miss me when I'm gone, but you will be fine. Write your thoughts in here, it will help."

He passed away on Christmas Eve. Christmas celebrations were cancelled, presents exchanged in silence and left unwrapped.

On the day of the funeral, her dad spoke to the mourners, regaling them with stories of the green fingered gardener, the loving husband, the patient, caring grandfather. Noticeable by its absence was any mention of the kind of a father he had been.

That night Suzy wrote in the journal for the first time, recording how sad and angry her dad appeared. As she wrote a putrid smell arose from out of the book, she gagged and threw it down. Gradually she understood.

She put her arms around her dad and told him "Grandad says he's so very sorry about making you eat all your food and for smacking you."

Her dad slowly lifted his head and cried huge gulping sobs but then after a while he seemed to calm and fall asleep. When he awoke, there was a change in him, and over the next few weeks he began to court his wife, they had never divorced, and he found he could understand her need for the closeness that he had never known how to give.

As the relationship grew, he began to talk about selling his dad's house to raise the funds to take them all on holiday. Suzy knew she was being selfish, but it upset her to think about strangers in the house. She expressed her dilemma in the journal. Once more a smell emanated from the pages, it smelled of burnt milk. Confused she tried to think what this could mean then recalled the first time she had used the microwave; she had attempted to make a cup of hot chocolate but mistakenly had pressed 30 minutes instead of seconds and then forgotten about it. The overwhelming smell had stayed with the microwave for several weeks. She went to the little oven and opened it, inside was a brown envelope containing her grandad's will leaving the house and all its contents to her and a letter to her dad saying all the things that he had found it impossible to say while he was alive. Why on earth had he put it there?

Perhaps in confusion as the morphine dulled the pain. He asked for forgiveness and told him to look in the wardrobe. He looked and found photographs that his father had taken of him over the years. Comments on the back of which demonstrated his pride in his son. Also, bank statements containing enough money to pay for a good holiday for the whole family.

Suzy found that whenever she wrote in the journal an aroma would emanate. When worried about an exam the smell of lavender arose to calm her nerves and she would inhale deeply. Sometimes the notes she wrote were not for her grandad, they were reminders of appointments or lectures or bills to pay. She began to write down her weight as she became aware that it was fashionable to be skinny and laughed when the smell of egg and bacon, fried onions, or bread straight from the oven permeated the room. Apparently, grandad loved her the way she was.

During her first year at university, her dad brought up the idea of selling the house once more suggesting that it would make sense to fund her education using the money, instead of applying for government loans, especially since she had become very fond of the life in Sheffield and would probably settle there. She wrote her thoughts in her journal and the musty smell of her grandad's garden shed arose.

She smiled, "What are you telling me now granddad?

The next half term she went back home and rooting through the shed found a manuscript for a book, she began to read and found it impossible to put down it was so gripping. Alongside the manuscript was a note addressed to her.

'I wrote this as I sat beside Lily's bedside watching her life slip away, I no longer have the inclination to take it further, but take it to a publisher for their opinion."

Suzy showed it to her dad and together they made enquiries. Within the year it was a best seller. The money raised helped fund university and encouraged her to put pen to paper herself. Whenever she had a mental block, she would turn to the journal for sensory inspiration and was never disappointed. Her work began to become noticed, and she revelled in the book signings where she always signed Suzy and Stanley Morrison.

An Everyday Story of Country Folk.

JUDITH BARRIE

'I have this talent for getting exactly what I want out of people,' Giles said, topping up his plate with extra potatoes.

'Yeah, right,' his sister said dismissively, 'That might work with a gullible nineteen-year-old girl, but Gran's a different kettle of fish. She's always been tight, but she's definitely been getting worse lately. You've no chance!'

They were sitting at the ancient wooden table in the kitchen eating their dinner. Giles liked a hearty meal when he came in from labouring in the fields, especially when there was a biting October wind gusting and it was threatening rain again. Samantha looked out of the window and saw her grandmother marching across the yard, heading for the kitchen door.

'She's here now. You can try out your winning system, but I bet you a fiver you won't get anywhere.' Giles, his mouth full of roast beef, didn't get chance to reply before his grandmother flung open the door, letting in a scurry of swirling brown leaves, and a draught that made smoke billow out of the fireplace.

'Hello, Gran,' he mumbled. 'Looks like rain again.'

'Did you get the top field ploughed?' she demanded. 'You've left it late for planting as it is, and we need that winter barley more than ever this year.' She pulled off her coat and went to the stove to make herself a hot drink.

Giles gave her his most sympathetic smile. 'It's half done, Gran, but the tractor conked out again. I'll get out to repair it as soon as I've had a bite to eat and get the ploughing finished before it gets dark.' A scowl was her only response. He continued cautiously. 'I was just saying to Samantha, Gran, I know it's the last thing we need at the moment, but, er, we really could do with a new tractor. It would pay dividends in the long run...'

'Just get it mended,' she said sternly, taking her mug of tea into the front parlour. 'Oh,' she said, as if an afterthought. 'I need to talk to you two tonight. I've got some, er, some...Something to tell you both...'

Samantha pulled out her tongue at Giles as Gran disappeared through the door.

'Told you,' she said, smirking, holding out her hand for a fiver she knew she would never get.

But Giles looked worried. 'What's all that about? "Something to tell you." I don't like the sound of that. At all!'

After tea, Gran dillied and dallied until Giles could stand no more. 'Well, spit it out, Gran. You've something on your mind and the suspense is killing me.'

Gran took a deep breath. She wasn't known for beating about the bush. 'I'm going to be wed again.' She drew herself up into the 'attack mode' that they knew so well. 'Now, don't go looking at me like that!' she said as their astonished faces rendered them dumb. 'Yer granddad's been dead these ten years, near enough,' (It was eight.) 'And he wouldn't have wanted me sitting weeping the rest of me life.' (He would.) 'Anyway, that's what's happening, so you'd better get used to the idea.' (He wouldn't.) She firmly clamped her jaws closed. As far as she was concerned that was the end of the matter.

'But...But who...?' stammered Samantha.

'But what about...? stammered Giles.

'It's Leonard Butterworth, if that's what you're trying to ask. And before you start, I know he's a bit younger than I am, but we're very well suited...'

'A *bit* younger! He's barely forty! You're nearly twice his age.' He went to pour himself a very stiff whisky.

'Len Butterworth! Master Baker!' Samantha said in disbelief. 'I mean, I know you're partial to his Battenburg, Gran, but...you can't marry him for his mince pies and custard tarts!'

Gran stood up furiously. 'I'll have you know, you two,' she said 'that's he's nearly forty-three. And I'm only seventy-four. You two should move with the times; a bit of a difference in ages doesn't matter a jot, not these days.'

If she'd had a feather boa, she would have tossed it round her neck as she stormed out of the room like a ship in full sail. Giles slumped into his chair and drained his whisky glass.

'Well! I never did,' said Samantha.

'No. And I hope you never do,' said Giles.

The news slowly sunk in and Gran announced that Leonard would be coming round for his dinner on Sunday, so that he could meet her grandchildren.

'Yeah, and no doubt have a good shuffty at what he's getting in the way of worldly goods,' said Giles bitterly.

Since his grandfather's sudden death eight years ago, Giles had kept the farm running with the help of a couple of labourers even though he had only been fifteen at the start. Now he felt himself fully in control of the whole operation: the small herd of Friesian cows along with the fearsome bullock, Charlie; the fields of potatoes and wheat; the small orchard of apples and plums; the extensive kitchen garden that provided most of their vegetables and herbs. He took a great pride in his work and looked forward to the day – although nothing had ever been formally discussed – when it would all belong to him. And Samantha, of course. She took care of all the paperwork side of things, the boring things like dealing with suppliers and keeping the accounts straight, while Giles loved to be outside with the wind blowing through his hair, the wonderful ripe, fruity farmyard smells in his nose. The thought of another man coming onto the scene...

'And where are they going to live? I suppose he'll move in here. Oh, God, can you imagine them in that front bedroom with her squeaky bed?'

Samantha screwed up her face in disgust. 'It doesn't bear thinking about,' she said.

'And, if she doesn't make a proper will, he'll cop the lot when she croaks. And she's bound to go first with thirty-odd years in his favour.' Giles had thought of nothing else for days.

'Oh, you're all heart, aren't you? 'Samantha said, sarcastically. 'But it's me you're talking to and I know you're nothing but a big leech, really, aren't you Giles?'

On Sunday morning Leonard Butterworth appeared with a bunch of flowers and a large paper bag of meat pies. Giles gazed mournfully out of the kitchen window and watched him park his shiny blue Ford next to Gran's farmyard-splattered maroon Mercedes. 'Oh, God!' he moaned.

Gran fluttered round like a love-sick teenager when Len came into the house. 'Oh, Leonard, you shouldn't have...' she said, hastily searching out a cut-glass vase from the back of a cupboard.

'No, you shouldn't have,' muttered Giles to Samantha. 'She hates lilies. She says the smell makes her feel sick.'

'And I bet those pies are leftovers from the shop yesterday,' Samantha said, distastefully eyeing the bag on the table.

'Lilies for my lovely Lillian!' Leonard said, beaming as he gave his fiancé a peck on the cheek.

'Don't know about the smell of *them* making me feel sick...' muttered Giles.

Eventually, the roast beef was served up and they all tucked in.

'Excellent beef! Is it your own?'

Samantha was watching, fascinated as his glasses bobbed up and down as he chewed.

'No,' said Giles. 'We're dairy.'

'But I suppose you could go into beef production.' This was met with an uncomfortable silence. Even Gran kept her head down, chewing. 'I believe it's very profitable.' More silence.

Eventually, Gran said: 'Giles, you could take Leonard a tour round the farm after dinner. That would be nice. Show him what's what.'

Giles mumbled something that could have possibly passed as an affirmation. So when the women were washing the dishes, Giles set out with Len, determined to walk the unfit, overweight, now over-stuffed little man off his feet. Len trotted along beside the lean and lanky Giles from one end of the farm to the other, firing questions when he could get his breath.

'So, what's the total acreage?'

'We don't count in acreage these days, 'said Giles scornfully. 'It's hectares. But it's about a hundred and fifty acres, I suppose.' It was, in fact, nearly two hundred.

'So, how much is an acre worth, say...?'

'Say. About five thousand an acre.' It was nearer seven.

'Did you know, you can build an average of sixteen houses per acre?'

'You don't say.'

'How much do you get in government subsidy?'

By the time they reached the house again, Len was looking decidedly peaky, but he just managed one last question as they approached the door. 'So, what is your cost/income ratio...?'

Giles crashed through the door into the warm kitchen, where the aroma of roast beef mingled with lilies to assault his nostrils. Gran was sitting at the table with Samantha, drinking tea.

'Oh, come in Leonard! You must be frozen! Come in and have a hot drink…'

'It started to rain,' he said peevishly, like a spoilt child, indicating his wet jacket.

Gran quickly ushered him in to the front parlour where a blazing fire and pot of tea were waiting. Giles slumped into a chair at the table.

'I swear to you, Sam, I will choke that little bastard!'

'Was it that bad?' she said, alarmed at Giles' scarlet cheeks.

'It's as plain as a turnip top, that, that…and you called *me* a leech! He's just after her money, Sam. All he's interested in is the bloody farm. He was even talking about building houses on that field near the woods…'

'No!' She looked as appalled as Giles. 'What are we going to do, Giles? What on earth are we going to do?'

The next few weeks were as bad as any Giles had ever known. To make matters worse, a vicious wind blew in from the north, tearing twigs from the trees and ripping the doors from the barn. Giles toiled from before dawn until after dusk, a permanent scowl on his face, his fingers numb with cold when he finally sat in the kitchen after tea, a large whisky in his hands, a fire roaring up the chimney.

Len always disappeared in the parlour with Gran when he came to visit, which was most nights. He had bought her a modest sapphire and diamond engagement ring, which she wore with great pride and she told them that they had set a date for the wedding just after Christmas.

'Our Gran!' said Samantha in disgust. 'Our Gran and Len Butterworth, master baker! Granddad would turn over in his grave if he knew about this.' (He would.)

On a Friday in early December, Gran announced that she had to go out, despite the icy weather, as she had some business to do with Mr. Shuttlecroft, her solicitor. Giles' stomach turned over. She was going to make a will! He was convinced of it.

'Gran, you mustn't go out in this! It's freezing. Can't it wait?'

'No. It cannot!' She had her best coat and hat on and furry gloves.

'Gran!' he implored, 'Are you sure you know what you're doing?'

She didn't even reply but opened the door and marched out, her best high heels clicking on the cobbles of the yard. Her begrimed Mercedes had been left out in the lane beyond the farmyard, which had become too icy to drive on.

Giles ran out after her, along with Samantha. 'Gran don't go out, you're going to slip if you're not careful!' shouted Sam. But Gran took no notice and carried on, going her own sweet way, determined, as ever.

She managed the cobbles in the yard without mishap, but as she was passing the slurry pit by the side of the barn, she stepped onto a half-frozen cow-pat and slipped straight onto her back, cracking her head on a cobble as she fell. Giles and Lesley looked on helplessly as she struggled to get up, but she toppled sideways into the slurry pit and slowly disappeared. They stood, transfixed, numbed, their mouths fixed open in perfect 'O's, paralysed with shock. As they stood there, a single feeble bubble popped on the surface and apart from the moaning wind, there was complete silence.

'Oh, God! What do we do?'

After a few moments of thought, Giles replied: 'Nothing. We do nothing, Sam. It's too late to do anything. There is no way she can be saved, so we do nothing.' He turned to her and took her hands into his. 'We go back into the house and we saw nothing. We know nothing. It's the only way.'

They walked slowly back to the house and slumped at the table. 'Let's just think about this, Sam. She was an old woman. About to hand over the farm to that slimy little toad. She must have had dementia to have even considered it in the first place.'

Samantha put her head in her hands and wept. 'And it was an accident anyway. Wasn't it? There was no way we could have got her out alive in any case.'

For the next couple of days they went about their business as best they could until the Monday evening, when the police appeared at the door.

'Are you Mr Giles Maybank?' asked the constable.

'Yes, I am, Officer. What can I do for you? If it's about that tree that's fallen in the lane, I'm going to get it moved tomorrow...'

'No Sir. We're enquiring into the whereabouts of Mrs Lillian

Maybank. She lives here, doesn't she?'

'Well, yes, she does, but now she's engaged to be married to Len Butterworth, she's been spending a lot of time there. Have you tried his shop?'

'Yes, sir. It was Mr Butterworth what reported her missing.'

'Oh. We just thought she was with Len. But now that you mention it, Officer, I was starting to wonder; she usually phones us most days for something…'

'When did you last see her?'

'Oh, it must have been, what, Saturday?' He turned to Samantha who had turned a whiter shade of pale. 'Oh, don't worry, Sam,' he said soothingly. 'She'll be…' But he couldn't think what on earth he could say that would be convincing and simply put on a worried face.

On Tuesday morning, Giles was in the yard when he saw Gran's body floating face down on the top of the slurry pit. He flew back to the house to tell his sister.

'Oh, no! Oh, no, No, no…'

'It's okay,' Giles said, 'We must report it to the police right away. Remember, it *was* an accident, and the police will see that when they examine the body. And if we'd not been there when it happened, we wouldn't have known she was in there, would we?'

Samantha sobbed while Giles phoned the police. Within an hour, the yard was filled with police cars and men in white suits crowding round the slurry pit, which was now covered by a canopy.

'I wonder what will happen to that sapphire ring?' asked Giles, watching from the kitchen window. 'I suppose they'll give it back to Butterworth.'

'I was right! You *are* a leech, Giles Maybank!' Samantha was still sobbing when Inspector Finch appeared at the door the next day. Giles offered him tea and they all sat at the table.

'I'm afraid I have some bad news for you,' he said bluntly. 'We have reason to believe that your grandmother was murdered.'

The gasps and sobs were genuine. Inspector Finch watched their reactions carefully. 'She has blunt force trauma to the back of her head which may have been the cause of her death.' He waited to assess their reactions.

Giles thought, *please, Sam, don't shout it out, she hit her head on the cobbles as she fell. Please don't.* (She didn't.)

He eventually left them, stunned again.

'You do realise, don't you, that we could be found guilty of her murder now! I can't believe what's happening to us. I just can't believe it. As next of kin, we'll inherit the farm and that gives us a motive. It can't have been bloody Butterworth, he had every reason to keep her alive until after the wedding!'

The next few days were torture. 'We'll have to run away!' Samantha sobbed.

'Don't get hysterical, Sam, we'll get through it. Somehow.'

There was a knock on the door. The Inspector was back.

Giles opened the door, defeated. 'Could I have a word with you, sir?' Inspector Finch asked brightly. 'And your sister too, if she's around?' Samantha burst into tears again as they all sat down at the table. It wasn't fair. It had been an accident. They must convince him that that was the truth. Her mind was so busy whirring that she was scarcely taking in the Inspector's words. But Giles did.

'Well, sir, it seems that we've got our man. We arrested Leonard Butterworth this morning for the murder of your grandmother. Apparently, three weeks ago he took out a *very* large insurance policy against her death, and he put in a claim for it yesterday. Even before we've released the body for burial.' He shook his head from side to side in disgust.

Giles didn't have to fake astonishment. 'Well, we thought he wanted to get his hands on the farm, but…'

'We can't find the weapon, but there's no doubt in our minds…And do you know, sir, he went to the undertaker's yesterday, with her hardly cold,' (A flagrant exaggeration.) 'and asked for the ring off her finger. He was afraid *you two* might get it!'

'Disgusting!' chorused the bereaved.

But they had learned their lesson and as the years went by Giles never again gave Samantha any cause to call him a big leech.

That Dratted Cat

That dratted cat, it's there again. It knows I can't get out.

It sits there in the garden, old and rather stout.

It torments me from dawn to dusk. It never moves an inch.

No matter how I snarl and growl, that cat just doesn't flinch.

I wonder what it thinks about, or if it thinks at all.

Does it know its lack of movement drives me up the wall?

My dream's come true, someone has left the front door open wide!

That fat cat's luck has just run out now I'm on the outside.

"Hey there, cat!", I growl at it, but still it doesn't move.

"Why don't you put up a fight? What are you trying to prove?"

But it just sat and stared right back. It showed no sign of fear.

Then just as I prepared to pounce a voice said "Rex, come here."

It startled me so much that in my shock I moved too fast.

I landed, splat! On that dratted cat, my game was up, alas!

As I landed, all I heard was an almighty crash

How was I to know that dratted cat was made of glass

MARY YOUNG

Ugly Old Bat

COLIN BALMER

Players: THOMAS : Mr Thomas, General Manager Bridgewaites
Undertakers

DOCTOR Dr Fritz Huegell - Psychotherapist

ROBERT 28-year-old driver for Bridgewaites

SCENE ONE

(SOUNDS OF WOODWORKING MACHINERY)

ROBERT: Mr Thomas, you wanted to see me.

THOMAS: Yes, come in Robert and close the door.

(MACHINERY NOISE REDUCES AND SOUND OF DOOR
CLOSING)

I want to discuss your future in the funeral service with
Bridgewaites.

ROBERT: Yes, sir. I've always done my best for the company. Is
everything OK?

THOMAS: You have driven for us for five years now and we would
like you to take a closer interest in our customers' needs.
You are a kind and sympathetic personable young man and
you should be looking at a future as a funeral director.
Driving a hearse should not be your ultimate ambition. How
old are you now?

ROBERT: I am twenty-eight, sir, and do want to get on. I have a wife
and daughter. But I get nervous near the widows or any old

lady in black. That's why I prefer to stay in the hearse. I would love to drive the new limousines. The '72 Silver Shadow launched this year must be the best car ever.

THOMAS: (CHUCKLES) I don't see Bridgewaites running a fleet of Rolls Royces soon – the seventies aren't being good to us. Anyway, back to you – When you have to collect the coffin, you hesitate if you have to go into the house where the deceased is laid out. Why do widows frighten you?

ROBERT: When I see them dressed in their mourning threads, I start to sweat and shiver and find it hard even to speak. My doctor has given me some tranquilizers if it gets too bad.

THOMAS: Popping pills is no answer. I was telling my wife about you and she says you should see her brother for psychotherapy. I have my doubts personally, but I promised her that I would let you decide. What do you think?

ROBERT: A shrink! Mr Thomas, I'm not crazy.

THOMAS: No, I am not saying that you are insane. He is not an NHS psychiatrist. She says he has been successful with hypnotherapy for a range of neuroses. Bridgewaites care about our staff and will pay the fees of course, so you really have nothing to lose. Could I make an appointment?

ROBERT: If you think it's best, sir. I will give it a try.

THOMAS: Very good Robert. I will make the arrangements. Now I think you have the Daimler to valet before this morning's service. Off you go young man.

SCENE 2

(BACKGROUND SOOTHING MUSIC)

THOMAS: Good morning, Fritz, or should I call you Doctor? You must be doing well with this posh clinic.

DOCTOR, Let's keep this on a professional standing, even though your wife made the appointment. It will also reassure our patient.

THOMAS: Patient? You know I wouldn't touch your kind of mumbo-jumbo quackery with a barge pole. The young man I employ can be helped with medication, but there's no future in that.

DOCTOR Science has moved on a long way since the medical professions turned to drugs to treat mental problems. I have a different approach.

THOMAS: Yes, I know. Robert is OK with drugs, but we cannot let him drive under the influence. We need a cleaner solution.

DOCTOR I told your wife about using hypnotherapy to identify patients' neuroses, then structuring an appropriate treatment plan without drugs. So, let's have Robert in.

(SOUND OF DOOR OPENING THEN CLOSING)

DOCTOR Hello, Robert. I'm Doctor Huegell. Together we will overcome your anxiety issues around little old ladies.

ROBERT: I hope so Doctor. Then I can drive a Bridgewaite limo for committals and cremation services.

DOCTOR Very good positive attitude. Please take off your coat and lie in the couch, breath deep and slowly. (PAUSE) Now Robert, I want to turn the clock back so we can investigate the source of your neuroses. First, I'll relax your mind then try to identify memories that may have caused the issues. Some people call it hypnotism. I like to think of it as deep relaxation.

ROBERT: That's why Mr Thomas sent me to you doctor.

DOCTOR Close your eyes and relax. (CALMLY) Ten... nine... eight... seven.... (FADES)

There's a white door in front of you marked 'Memories.' Push it open. What can you see? How do you feel?

ROBERT: I'm in my late teens; the sun is shining in your garden. My transistor radio is playing Radio Caroline. I'm stretched out on the grass with a drink of Dad's home brew. This is Sunday my day off – I feel glad to be alive.

DOCTOR: Good. Something happens to spoil the feeling, what is it?

ROBERT: There's the old widow from two doors down coming towards me, waving her arms and shouting. She's short and fat - dressed all in black. I think she's on her way home from chapel. (LOUD) Oy missus, you can't just waltz into our garden – That's trespassing! She's screaming that the radio's too loud for a Sunday morning. Oy! Get lost! Stop it! You can't do that. That's my tranny radio. I don't believe

70

it! She's stabbed my radio with her umbrella and smashed it against the garden wall.

DOCTOR: How does this make you feel?

ROBERT: I'm incredibly angry and frustrated. I can't do anything now because she plays bingo with my Mam. I'll get my revenge on the ugly old bat when I get older. I hate old biddies like that.

DOCTOR: Hmm, an interesting experience. Now let's take you further back say to when you were ten. What are you doing?

ROBERT: Me and my mates play footy every day. There's eight or nine of us playin.' My team is United and we are winning City three none. We're playing on the green at the end of the Avenue. Jumpers and coats are the goal posts. Gerry Mac passes to Tommo. I run into the penalty box. Tommo gives me the ball. 'Ave it! I score a blinder past Jimmy Eck. Four none. Four none. Four none. Yeh! We all shout and dance. Oh No! The balls gone into someone's garden. It's my goal so I have to get it. Do I knock on the door or chance jumping the hedge and get it? Tommo shouts 'Hurry up.'

DOCTOR: Why does he say that?

ROBERT: Someone might come out and nick our ball. But I'm too slow. The door opens and an old lady in a black frock and cardigan comes out. She's got a black veil on as well. I ask, 'Can I have my ball back missus?' She glares at me, and she grabs the ball. Oh No! She's stabbed the ball with the scissors she is holding. She shouts 'Go and play where you live. I don't want you making all your noise around here. Learn some respect for the deceased.'

DOCTOR: What did she mean?

ROBERT: When I go back home my mam told me that the old lady's husband died the week before and she was in mourning.

DOCTOR: How did you feel then?

ROBERT: We didn't know. She still shouldn't have popped our ball. We were doing no harm. I'll get my own back on the ugly old bat on mischief night.

DOCTOR: I see there's a bit of a pattern developing here. Let's go further back now. Can you remember when you were very young?

ROBERT: I'm in my pram on holiday. The sun is shining. I've been fed and winded. I've got a lovely warm wet feeling in my nappy. Just lying here gurgling and chuckling. I am one very happy baby. What's this? A horrible face leans over, all dark and sinister looking. I'm frightened and cry out. The pram starts bouncing and I'm bumped against the sides. I cry louder.

DOCTOR: It seems someone is trying to rock you to sleep.

ROBERT: Now, I'm being bounced about the pram. I don't like this and scream out to say so. She shouts back 'Be quiet, horrible little brat.' When I grow up I'll remember to avoid these ugly old bats.

DOCTOR: That's enough for this session. I want to bring you out of your hypnosis. Focus on your breathing let the personalities you remember drift into the past. Now come back to your physical body. Count with me one, two, three, four,

ROBERT: five, six, seven eight nine ten. Wow doctor, I feel great now, lighter, refreshed and so calm.

DOCTOR: You told me a lot about your antipathy to old ladies. I need to think about where we go next time. I have confidence we will overcome your fear as well. Book an appointment with my receptionist for another therapy session.

ROBERT: Thanks, doctor I'll see you next time. 'Bye.

(SOUND OF DOOR OPENING THEN CLOSING)

SCENE 3

(SOUND OF DOOR OPENING THEN CLOSING)

DOCTOR: Make yourself comfortable Robert. You will remember the technique from last week's visit. Breathe slowly and easily. Close your eyes and count with me, (LOW) ten, nine, eight

ROBERT: eight, seven, six …. (FADES)

DOCTOR: Today I want to regress you to a former life and want you to tell me what you see and experience. We're going back to a time before you were born and somewhere different. Picture yourself in late nineteenth century somewhere you might have been on holiday. Tell me where you are.

ROBERT: I'm in a large Victorian house on top of the hill overlooking the fishing port of Whitby. I can smell the fish, ships and the sea. It's the middle of the night.

DOCTOR: Good. What are you doing?

ROBERT: I'm alone in a massive four poster bed. The room is cold, Rose my maid, has let the fire die down for the night. I'm a young maiden of nineteen with jet black hair flowing over my shoulders. I'm wearing a beautiful embroidered white nightdress.

DOCTOR: Do you have a name?

ROBERT: I'm Nancy, the elder daughter of Lord Robert Vickers. Wait! Something wakes me. I'm shivering with the cold and see the heavy curtains billowing into the room. Rose must have left the window open. I will reprimand her in the morning. I bury myself deeper in the blankets to get warm. I hear an owl hoot and wings flapping.

DOCTOR: How are you feeling?

ROBERT: I feel safe and warm under the sheets, but I'm shivering with fear of something going to happen.

DOCTOR: Do you know what you are afraid off?

ROBERT: No, I'm simply scared. What! The curtain is opening – I can see the dark night sky lit by a full moon. How did the curtain open? There is no draught. Look - a black shape is silhouetted against the moon. It is not the owl I just heard. **What is it? What can it be**? It is flying and its size suggest it might be a crow - somehow vile and malevolent. But not

74

at night surely? I peer through the darkness and recognise the outline of a large bat. Now I'm terrified. I try to hide myself under the covers – A scream won't come no matter how wide I open my mouth. Shut my eyes tight and cover them with my hands and it will go away. All goes quiet as I tremble under the blanket. Thank God, it's gone.

DOCTOR: Push back the covers. Look around the room. Tell me what you see.

ROBERT: A rectangle of moonlight in the middle of the floor. Every corner is pitch black. I can't make out anything other than the fluttering curtain. (PAUSE) Wait a minute, there is something at the side of the bed – Oh No! No No. the bat that came in has morphed into a human shape. He's all in black with a black cape. No! I can see more now. He comes closer and leans over me. His eyes glow like red hot coals. His bloody lips curl back in a sinister smile. I can see sharp fangs glistening white. I want to move away but I'm paralysed. My own weight pins me - rigid - to the bed. **Help. Don't come closer. I can't stop him.** He bends forward to kiss me. No, not kiss. I feel the sharp delicious pain as his fangs pierce my jugular vein. I'm falling asleep as I feel my blood being drained from me. The room fades and oblivion beckons. Even the crisp moonlight is washed out to a grey dark shimmering cloud. (FADES)

DOCTOR: Robert where are you? (PAUSE) Robert can you answer me? (PAUSE) Robert come back.

ROBERT: Who! Where? Oh! What?

DOCTOR: You were drifting away into a coma. Where are you now?

ROBERT: I'm, I'm feeling a bit woozy. It's morning. Ouch! My neck hurts. There's blood on my fingers when I touch the weeping sore. There's not a sign of the black demon from last night. **Hello! Who's there?** Oh, good morning, Rose. I, I, I don't feel very well this morning – I think I'll take my breakfast in bed. Rose goes to the window and throws open the curtains. An explosion of golden light as the low sun climbs over the horizon and floods my room.   **Ouch!** I feel a stabbing pain in my neck as its rays touch me. The pain is spreading all over. The hurt increases and fills my frail body. It gets worse – my whole being feels aflame, blistered and sun scalded. The unbearable agony - overwhelms not just my physical but also my spiritual presence completely. I'm losing consciousness. (PAUSE) The pain eases. I'm floating upwards. I look down on of the bed (SCREAM) – the girl's body is charred and blackened – the bedclothes are untouched. I look away from the horrible sight toward a brilliant welcoming white light...

The - ugly - old – bat – has – killed - me.

[SILENCE]

DOCTOR: Robert (PAUSE)   Robert? (PAUSE) **Robert!** (PAUSE)

I'm now going to bring you back to your physical self. Take deep breaths and follow me as I count you back in, to reality. One, Two, Three (FADES) and ten. Open your eyes.

ROBERT: Wow doctor I've never felt so relaxed and refreshed. Am I cured now?

DOCTOR: No, we have just identified the source of your neurosis. I'll put together a remedial course of therapy and managing strategy. But remember a drop of anxiety is the oil that lubricates the gears of the problem-solving machinery in your mind. Go now and look forward to driving those luxury vehicles.

ROBERT: Thank you doctor.

(SOUND OF DOOR OPENING THEN CLOSING)

SCENE 4

(MUTED SOUNDS OF DRINKS PARTY)

ROBERT: Have a long and happy retirement Mr Thomas. (GLASSES CHINK) You've been a good boss and my best friend over the last thirty odd years.

THOMAS: Thank you Robert. I'm sure I leave Bridgewaites Funeral Directors in your very capable hands. It is because of you that we have an enviable reputation for client care and compassion. It's amazing really when we think back to your problems all those years ago. In spite of my reservations, the hypnotherapy worked well, didn't it?

ROBERT: Yes, indeed. But hypnotism was only the beginning. The resolution started with a period of immersion therapy. Do you know that, after reading Bram Stoker's novel, I watched nothing but vampire films for months and months? Eventually my subconscious accepted that they are not

77

invincible, (LAUGHS) nor are little old widows their contemporary manifestations.

THOMAS: I think the therapy went further than that though, didn't it?

ROBERT: (LAUGHS) I suppose you're talking about my anxiety coping programme?

THOMAS: Yes, of course. Everyone at Bridgewaites knows you as the driver who always carries a crucifix to all services (LAUGHS) …and there's always a lingering aroma of garlic in whichever car you have driven.

THOMAS AND ROBERT: Cheers

(SOUND OF CHINKING GLASSES)

Old Boots

These tired old boots
of well-worn rand
have carried me
across the land

Through:
vale and valley
Dale and dell
Stream and River
Moor and Fell

Through:
Scent of Spring
and Summer Breeze
Autumn mist
and Winter freeze

I've walked them all
So, truly blessed
these tired old boots
now need a rest!

WARREN DAVIES

Archie & E_{II}R

ROSEMARY SWIFT

My husband Archie first saw Queen Elizabeth II in the 1950s when she was visiting the Northwest. As she passed by, he was struck by what a beautiful complexion she had.

[On another occasion, he was struck by how orange was the complexion of Yuri Gagarin as he passed by Archie on a visit to Manchester on 12 July 1961 as a guest of the Union of Foundry Workers, being a foundry worker before becoming a cosmonaut. At that time, Archie was also a foundry worker but kept *his* feet firmly on the ground.]

Archie was to meet Queen Elizabeth II more closely on Tuesday, 14 November 2006 at Buckingham Palace and have a chat with her when awarded the MBE for his work with Salford Lads & Girls Club. With son and daughter, I accompanied Archie and had a hectic couple of days in London. Stephen Wright, the photographer of the iconic picture of The Smiths taken outside the entrance of Salford Lads & Girls Club met us and took some lovely snaps including those when we went for afternoon tea at the Houses of Parliament at the invitation of the then Salford MP Hazel Blears.

Archie was whisked away from us on arrival at Buckingham Palace and we other three made our way to the Investiture Room. As we hurried along corridors I lost a shoe. *"Oh"*, I tittered as I retrieved it *"I feel like Cinderella."* *"More like one of the ugly sisters"* daughter Cath whispered to her brother Tom. Charming! But no Prince! We were so prompt we ended up on front row left so was able to see Archie behave impeccably doing everything correctly as directed.

[The actor Charles Dance received his knighthood that day and was very dignified unlike a lady who nervously forgot to curtsy and a shabbily dressed mad scientist type who accidentally turned his back on the Queen.]

We returned home to host, the following Sunday, a large celebratory party at St. Luke's Parish Centre at Irlams o'th' Height coinciding with the baptism of our third grandchild, Jessica. Now aged 16, she is the one out of our four grandchildren to volunteer at Salford Lads & Girls Club – probably meant to be as Archie now aged 88 in his 77th year of SLC membership is too frail to make further contributions but the Club is still in his soul and a place he loves to visit as often as possible.

King & I

ROSEMARY SWIFT

As I pen this on Remembrance Sunday 2022, I reflect on King Charles III (then the Prince of Wales) passing by me and husband Archie on 1 July 2006 at the Thiepval Memorial in France on the 90th anniversary of the Battle of the Somme. We were there in memory of my Great Uncle and my husband's Uncle, both named on the memorial as casualties of World War One.

On the next occasion our paths crossed, King Charles did not pass me by but altered his prompted course to chat with me. On 4 February 2010 at Salford Lads & Girls Club, representatives from all youth groups circled the gymnasium. Lined up at one end of the Junior Games Room, were the then Salford MP Hazel Blears, the then Leader of Salford City Council Barbara Spicer, other dignitaries and my husband Archie as a recipient of the MBE for his work with SLC. After this welcoming committee, curving around the wall were senior SLC officers, some young Club members and, skulking by the drinks machine, hiding behind the open door, were four wives of the Officers, including yours truly.

As HRH The Prince of Wales and HRH The Duchess of Cornwall arrived with their entourage they were ushered into the Junior Game Room but instead of going straight across to dignitaries, Prince Charles took a sharp turn left (deliberately I suspect) ending up face to face with me. "_So, who are you then?_" he asked.

Not sure what to say as we wives were not supposed to be introduced to him, I answered "_oh, we are the WAGS._"

Well, Hazel Blears tried to stifle a laugh not very successfully. Thankfully, she had time to recover as Prince Charles proceeded to talk to the youth of the Club, then Club Officers before reaching the top-nobs.

All parties then moved to the gym where Charles and Camilla inspected a very large circle of youths representing such as Army Cadets, Boys Brigade, Boy Scouts, Girl Guides, Sea Cadets, etc. Eventually, Prince Charles sat at a small table where again us four wives were just on the other side of the netting so were able to hear him say to Camilla as he was signing a document declaring he had been there that day: "_what date is it?_" - She answered but not very loudly so he asked again: "_it's blah, blah, blah_" she shouted. Very much a married couple!.

The Girl with the Flaxen Hair.

JUDITH BARRIE

Detective Inspector Finch leaned back in his chair and linked his hands behind his neck, a smug expression on his face.

'You're looking chuffed with yourself this morning, sir.' Sergeant Reynolds put the coffee on his boss's desk: black with three and a quarter sugars. Fussy bugger, D.I. Finch.

'Yeah. Nearly four years he's done. The Painter. He only got eight, so I suppose he'll be out wandering the streets again soon. But I'll be there! I'll watch every move he makes, ready to pounce. First safe he puts his sticky fingers on and I'll have him back inside, Reynolds, quick as a flash. Mister Franswar bloody Debewsie.' He grinned at the Sergeant, who left the room nodding. But it had taken D.I. Finch over five years to catch this ace safecracker the first time; this yeggman with the sticky fingers.

Meanwhile, Francois de Bussy was lying on his bunk, staring at the ceiling and counting the days to his release. About three months to go, he reckoned, and he was thinking back to the time when he'd been nicked by the Inspector after a cat and mouse chase that had lasted, oh, about five years.

The gang had all scarpered, leaving Frankie holding the baby, only this baby was jelly and about to kick off any minute. The Inspector had a beaming smile on his face as he got the handcuffs out, until about two seconds later when they both had their eyebrows removed in the blast. But it was a fair cop, Frankie had thought later, and to tell the truth he was fed up with the gang and their coarse language, filthy habits and thieving ways. Mick was the worst. It was Mick who had given him the nickname, The Painter.

'Wot'cher called?' he'd said when Frankie told him his name for the first time, 'Debewsie? E's that painter chap, ain't 'e? Frank the bloody painter!'

'No, Debussy is a composer, not a painter. And I'd prefer it if you'd call me Frankie.'

'Bloody 'ell! Right, Frankie it is then!'

Philistines, the lot of them, Frankie thought.

But 'The Painter' stuck and all the gang called him that, and then later the police.

His full name was Francois de Bussy and he was twenty-six years old now after wasting the last four in the slammer. Frankie didn't like it in prison: he had to share his cell with a variety of uncouth individuals, the worst being the present incumbent, Freddie 'Fingers' MacDonald, who was in on a similar charge to his own: safe cracking. Frankie had gained quite a reputation in the underworld for his slender, nimble fingers and Freddie constantly badgered Frankie for tips, but had about as much success picking Frankie's brain as he'd had picking locks outside – not much.

The rest of the inmates were just as bad, but at least he wasn't forced to listen to them snoring and snorting every night in the bunk below or farting half the night on the 'in-cell sanitation facility', the way he had to listen to Freddie. This happened whenever they'd had anything green in the meal, which was just about every day.

'Wotchya got planned when yer get out, Frankie?' Freddie had asked him.

'I just want to be free.'

'Yer goin' over to that old grannie o' yours in France?'

'I hope so.'

In fact, Frankie knew exactly what he wanted to do when he got out; he dreamed about it almost every night, and most nights he wasn't even asleep. He closed his eyes and he could envisage a field full of wheat, scattered about with scarlet poppies and a girl in a blue summer dress running through it, skipping and waving her arms with the sheer joy of life. Her long, flaxen hair was streaming behind her as she ran effortlessly under the hot blue sky of Provence. In the distance was his grandmother's house, squatting comfortably after three centuries, the chickens squabbling in the herb garden and a pot of soup on the fire, waiting.

On the bunk below Freddie let go of a real stinker. 'How about that Frank? That was a real belter, wannit?'

'A belter, Freddie.' Only two months to go and he would have forgotten Freddie's name within a week.

Frankie had been before the parole board and it had been agreed that he would be released on the fifteenth of July, with the strict understanding that he would report to the probation officer twice a week. Fine. No problem. Frankie's behaviour had been exemplary for four years and, much as they would have liked to, they could find no reason to prolong his stay.

Two weeks before his release, Tommy Barnes came to visit.

'Right,' said Tommy, 'What do yer want me to do?'

'I want you to rent me a clean, decent room. Somewhere on a busy road, lots of yellow lines outside, not easy to park, if you get my drift.'

'Yeah, yeah!'

'I want a pink suitcase and a set of women's' clothes, size fourteen. Something real pretty and girly.' Tommy was at a loss for words. 'And now this is important Tommy, a really high-class blonde wig. Pale blonde. Like mine would be if they'd not shaved my head. And I want real hair, not plastic muck.'

Tommy sat, bemused. 'I think I'm getting the idea, Frank. You think you can pull it off?'

'Yeah, I'm sure I can. Now, have I got enough in my piggy bank to cover that?'

'Yeah, sure. That last caper done good; you got sixty thou.'

'Right. Put all the gear in the room when you've rented it and when you pick me up, we can drive straight there.'

On the morning of the fifteenth of July, Detective Inspector Finch was in a sombre mood. 'Right, Reynolds, Get down to the 'Scrubs, I want you on The Painter's tail the second he gets out through the door. I want to make sure the address he's given us is right one - the same one he's given probation.'

'Yes, sir.'

Frankie was nervous as he came into contact with the fresh air of the outside world for the first time in four years. Tommy was waiting with the car and they sped off so fast that Reynolds almost lost them.

'Everything ready as requested, Frankie. Great idea of yours to dress up as a woman, and Fisher Street is chocka all day long, so the Bill won't notice when you slip out. I got a blue coat and dress from Marks and Sparks, just like you asked for.'

'Thanks, Tommy.'

'That wig cost nearly a grand!'

'I know. It'll be worth it though. And once I'm over the other side, if you ever fancy a holiday down in the Val de Loire, my old gran will see you right.'

Sergeant Reynolds had got snaggled up in the traffic on Fisher Street and didn't get to see the number where Frank had been dropped, but it was probably the flat over the massage parlour. Well, he'd been in the slammer a long time…

Frankie dutifully went to see his probation officer for the first few weeks before he made his move. Every detail had been checked with Tommy, who was going to drive him down to the Channel ferry, so on the morning of the first of September, Frankie put on the new clothes and the thousand pound wig and looked at himself in the mirror. Free at last. His grandmother would understand. She'd always understood him, when he hadn't wanted to play rough games with the boys, when he would prefer to spend hours reading to her by the fire after her glasses broke and she couldn't afford to have them repaired.

The passport wasn't much of a problem – Francois de Bussy easily passed for a girl's name to the average Englishman, and his fair hair had almost been down to his shoulders when the photo had been taken. And the French were open-minded enough to accept all manner of deviations in these matters. The journey went smoothly and Frankie could only imagine D.I.Finch, hopping mad, shouting and bawling, 'What the hell do you mean, Reynolds? He disappeared? He bloody can't have!'

His grandmother was expecting him and would have his old room ready. He had enough money to keep them in luxury for a few years and, anyway, he hoped to set up his own little business in the village. He'd always been good with his hands, but instead of twiddling knobs to crack safes, he would apply them to woodwork. He could make chests of drawers, kitchen chairs, tables, maybe even the odd wardrobe or dresser…

A few weeks later and the villagers had already become accustomed to the sight of a happy young woman, dressed in blue, running through the wheat fields in the September sunshine, her flaxen hair streaming in the wind.

Difference

The leaves on this tree are so different
Yet are they also the same?

I reach out - examine more closely,
Feel them - as shapes without name.

Fatter or slimmer,
Thicker or thinner.
Weaker or stronger,
Shorter or longer.

Pointed or rounded
Smaller or larger.
Softer or sharper,
Paler or darker.

Harmony, blended,
As nature intended.
Each one resplendent,
in its unique way.

The leaves on the same tree are different,
As, ever human, are we!

SYLVIA EDWARDS

Fire on the SS Australis

JOHN NEWTON

I was fascinated to read the history of the Australis, she certainly was a grand lady. I had the pleasure of her company twice, once as a 15-year-old boy travelling in March 1968 voyage 13 southbound, and then again in the Oct 1975 when I travelled on voyage 51 northbound. I have many fond memories of the people and events I experienced while sailing on her, but on the sea, as on the land, life is not always plain sailing and one quickly realises when life itself is threatened how vulnerable we are. Fortunately for all on board that day, the captain and crew who sailed on this voyage were very professional, disciplined and brave to the extent that every man, woman and child on board were delivered safely to their destination. Some were delivered not in the way they expected, others were better for their experience, and some I dare say vowing never to set foot on a ship again. My mother, eldest sister Heather, younger brother David and sister Angela were boarding the S. S. Australis at Southampton, we were going to join our father in Australia. En route our journey would be calling in Dubrovnik and Greece to pick up immigrants who were going out to Australia to start a new life. It was then sailing on to Cape Town, South Africa, then across to Mauritius and finally Fremantle.

Come back with me now onto the deck of SS Australis. The year is 1968 the date March 13.

It was a glorious day on deck; as the ship cut her way through the South Atlantic Ocean to the next port of call, Cape Town. The familiar chime of the tannoy sounded throughout the ship, announcing lunch would be served in the Atlantic dining room.

I had arranged with my mother and sister that straight after lunch we would take in the first showing of the film, "The Sons of Katie Elder" starring John Wayne. The cinema was situated towards the front of the ship on A Deck and it was here, whilst leaving the cinema just before the interlude, that I sensed something was not quite right. There was the distinct smell of smoke and my first thought was that the immigrants didn't like the food on board and must be cooking in their cabins.

I turned out of the cinema, travelled a short distance along the passageway and was surprised to see the heavy fire door closed. I thought maybe this was a prank; after all you only had to be tall enough to throw the switch above the fire door to close it. As I got closer to this door I could see smoke, and I could hear the panic in raised voices. I returned to the cinema thinking we could not be on fire, yet knowing we were. As a young boy I had seen enough English films to know that an Englishman is always calm in situations like this, but I could feel the panic rising. I made it back to where my mother and sister were sitting and said to my mother in a low voice, "We have to get out of here. The ship's on fire".

She didn't have time to answer me as someone stuck their head around the door, and in a very loud voice screamed "Fire, Fire!"

People got to their feet quickly and started to exit the cinema. Most were standing when the helmsmen put the ship very hard to starboard. I can tell you, some thirty odd years later, I still see and feel the extent of the roll, in fact I really thought we were going completely over. The emergency fire alarms deafeningly loud rang in our ears. With their own sense of urgency, they resounded in every corner of the ship.

By this time, the fire had spread to the upper decks travelling through the concealed ceilings spaces into some of the public rooms. I believe the captain realised the danger of the fire being fanned throughout the upper structures of the ship and took the evasive action to put her about, out of the wind and stopped the ship.

Leaving the cinema, we made our way up the stairway in semi darkness, where we got caught up in a mass of panicking people all with the one objective to get out as quickly as possible to the open decks. In the push and shove of things I lost contact with Mum and Heather.

I remember quite vividly finding myself beside an elderly gentleman in his late 70's trying to make his way up the stairs among all the pushing and shoving. My instinct, spurred on by panic, was to go on past him. He looked so vulnerable there among all this chaos, so I turned to him and asked if he was ok and did he need assistance to get up the stairs.

In a very calm reassuring voice he said, "I am alright, get yourself up topside son."

I believe he must have been the calmest person on those stairs that day.

All the ships alarm bells were still ringing, as we made our way on to the open deck. I managed to find my mother and sister, and to our despair my younger brother David (9 years old) and sister Angela (7 years old) could not be found anywhere on the deck, so we assumed they must still be below deck in our cabin 170 on upper deck. Try to imagine the scene that day. The aft decks are absolutely full of passengers and a few had completely lost their composure. I could see a man crying, an officer with his lifejacket on and a spare one in his hand as he addressed us with a megaphone from the top of the Sports Deck. He told us not to panic because, on the horizon off to starboard, the P&O liner Canberra was coming to our assistance.

While frantically looking for my siblings I bumped into my friend, Jack, and his father, an ex-Royal Navy man, who told me that if we must abandon ship to go for the inflatables as they are much safer. This filled me with even more panic and an urgency to find my brother and sister but the crew on the starboard side would not let me back into that part of the ship. The high-pitched voices of the Greek crew ringing in my ears, "Too Dangerous! Too Dangerous.."

I then tried to gain entry on the Port Side of the ship and got the same response. In desperation I pretended to walk away, before quickly turning around, I raced back, jumping over the fire hoses as I dodged the crew and entered the ship from the Promenade Deck. With adrenaline pumping I jumped the steps two and three at time and quickly reached the bottom of the second set of stairs where it was eerily silent. To my surprise no one had followed me down. I looked at the long passageway filled with acrid smoke, which made me gag from thick phlegm gathering in my mouth and throat..

Moving along the corridor I saw the little red emergency lights fitted to the ceiling dimly visible shrouded in smoke. There was complete silence and not a soul to be seen. The alarm bells had fallen silent. The thought passed through me fleetingly that the alarms had ceased because everyone had left the ship to a safe area. This filled me with more anxiety.

There was not a soul to be seen as I made my way along the passageway to the cabin, you could have heard a pin drop. I remember thinking to myself what if they are not here, where do I look for them, who can help me find them in this huge ship and among all this danger and chaos.

I finally reached Cabin 170 where my sister and brother were sitting on the top bunk. They didn't seem to be aware of the emergency and the cabin had relatively little smoke in it compared to the passageways. I quickly scooped up the lifejackets and warm coats for everyone. I told my brother and sister we must attend boat drill, I must have not been thinking clearly with that statement as it would become quite obvious once we went into the passageways that this was no drill. We made it safely up to the top decks, to my mother's immense relief. We stayed there for some time not knowing our fate.

Eventually the fire was put out and we were informed a crew member had sadly lost his life fighting the fire. I cannot remember how long we stood up on the deck, only to say it was a very long time. Most people on the aft decks that day would certainly remember the large albatross that circled above us, about the same time we were being informed the fire was under control. The bird is known in legend as a mariner's protector of souls, it certainly was a sailor's good omen on that day.

That night with limited emergency lighting and no air conditioning we drifted along. Some of the ship's public lounges were used for the passengers to sleep in. I remember walking into the very large Smoking Room at the front of the ship. It was in the early hours of the morning at about 1.30 am, where people were lying down wherever they could in the dimly lit room. I noticed a lot of the passengers were not yet asleep, but the strangest thing was the silence. Nobody spoke or stirred, it was as if the whole room was suspended in time. As I reached the front of the room I could hear the wind gently moaning as it passed through the opened windows, pushing the heavy gold curtains aside. I stood there for some time listening only to the wind, even the reassuring gentle vibrations of the ship's engines was absent as we drifted along. It was such a surreal experience that even today, I can return to that room as if it were only yesterday and stand there on the port side listening to the wind, aware of the complete silence of the room behind me.

I'm not quite sure if we were one or two days out from Cape Town when the fire had taken hold, but I do remember seeing some of the damage the fire had caused to the ceilings in some of the public rooms. Most of the paint had been burnt off Australis` large funnel and there was a lot of damage on her lower decks as the fire had initially started in her engine room. When you cast your eyes to her forward bow area, the deck here was stacked three feet high with every conceivable fire extinguisher.

My friend Danny, who was a crew member, was busy painting the ships funnel the following day after the fire. He told me he was very tired and had little sleep in the last twenty-four hours. He had been firstly fighting the fire for many, many hours before we passengers became aware of the emergency, then cleaning up and now the funnel had to be ship shape before the captain would take her into Cape town.

We reached Cape Town safely and received quite a welcome. An ambulance was stationed at the side of the ship to take off a lady who had gone into premature labour. This turned out to be a joyous occasion for Mr. and Mrs. L. Iokimidis, who gave birth to a healthy baby in a Cape Town hospital. They then re-joined the ship and sailed on to Australia.

I remember eating with paper plates and plastic knives and forks under make do spotlights in the Atlantic dining room. Many passengers were angry with these conditions, Chandris the ships' owners flew some of these people on to their destination in Australia. We decided to stay on the Australis while she was being repaired. It took about 5 days, and in this time we had a bit of a mutiny of sorts, when all the stewards walked off the ship. This was because the captain wanted to sail before they felt that adequate repairs had been done. We finally did set sail, but many of the passengers, especially those from the lower decks would not sleep below, they slept on deck chairs up on the Promenade Deck all the way to Australia and no coaxing could get them below deck.

The circumstances I found myself in those ensuing hours of danger and the days that followed were and still are priceless to me. On that day I learned much, along with the knowledge that panic driven on by the will to live can be contagious and at times dangerous. Keep Calm at all costs. The will of others to protect life at all costs is a most marvellous uplifting human trait. Never take a single day of life for granted, life can be short.

I settled in Australia, married my wife Allison and in the October of 1975 I introduced her to another fine lady the S. S. Australis. We honeymooned on board the ship on voyage 51 northbound, Fremantle to England via the Panama Canal.. Allison and I started our life as newlyweds on Australis, seeing many wondrous parts of the world. Our son Clifton was conceived on her.

I would like to say how fortunate I was to experience this fine ship, firstly as a young boy then as an adult. The ship, the people and the places are a part of my life. My father Garfield Newton sailed on her to the shores of Australia to forge out a new life for his family

The good ship Australis brought so many people together and forged lifelong friendships and good will wherever she sailed.

Australis no longer sails the vast oceans of the world she lays peacefully on the floor of the Atlantic Ocean of the coast off Fuerteventura in the Canary Islands. Her oceans are now our mind -0 her spirit sails on entwined.

Memories

These faded fruits
No longer ripe
Are gathering dust
For me to wipe.

The forgotten steps
I need to trace
Another time
Another place.

I try to clench
These grains of sand
Slipping slowly
Through my hand.

A shimmering wraith
Of time gone by
Dreams and desires
Now dormant lie.

WARREN DAVIES

Sachertorte

JUDITH BARRIE

There were dozens of coffee shops in Vienna in the 1950s, but none so famous and revered as Cafe Demel on Stephansplatz. The pastrycook, Georg, had spent three decades perfecting his masterpiece, *Sachertorte*, and now people flocked from all over the city - all over Austria, in fact - to indulge in this spectacular confection. First concocted by Franz Sacher in 1832 for his employer, the statesman Prince Klemens von Metternich, at Demel's Georg had tweaked the recipe a little here, and a little there and the results were daily displayed in the front window of the coffee shop for all the world to see and wonder at. A slice neatly cut on a delicate porcelain plate at the side, showed the perfection of the glossy chocolate topping, the perfect texture of the sponge and the evenness of the apricot filling, bringing gasps of delight from the eager customers, who would rush into the shop and order a large slice, accompanied by a dollop of *schlagobers* - whipped cream - and, of course, a cup of espresso. Ahhh

Meanwhile, a hundred yards away on Herrengasse, the Cafe Braunerhof was likewise doing a brisk trade. Madame Schneider brushed wisps of hair from her brow as the last customer left the cafe and she heaved a sigh of impatience. Where was that girl? Kristina had been with her for almost four years now and had proved to be hard-working and polite, but since she had taken on the new pastry-cook, Bernhard, after her husband had died, Kristina had taken to sloping off to the kitchens, to 'help him'!

In the kitchen Kristina was preparing the cake pans for *Sachertorte*, first lining them with paper, before *very* lightly buttering them and giving them the *merest* dusting of flour, just as Bernhard had shown her. She watched, entranced, as Bernhard stirred the melting chocolate, then beat the egg yolks with a fork, before folding them into the chocolate together with melted butter and vanilla essence. His handsome face was lined in deep concentration, his moustaches twitching up and down as he worked. Bernhard was twenty-four and Kristina thought he had the most beautiful brown eyes in the whole world. They reminded her of chocolate doughnuts, filled with vanilla cream – ooh, delicious.

He took some apricot jam on the edge of a silver spoon and turned to Kristina, who opened her mouth like a little bird, blushing as pink as cherry blossom. 'Mmmm,' she said, 'What have you put in it, Bernhard? That is not plain apricot jam.'

He smiled at her. 'Ah,' he said, 'it is my secret. Maybe one day I will tell you.' Now she blushed as pink as a ripe strawberry.

'Kristina!' Madame Schneider's voice was sharp as a pistol shot. 'I need you behind the counter. Now!'

'I was just...'

'Don't give me "I was just..." Counter! Now!'

Kristina scurried back into the shop, just in time to serve a customer, the doorbell still jingling. She took the order and dashed back into the kitchen to ask Bernhard for a plate of hot apricot pancakes and then busied herself extracting a cup of espresso from the new machine – Madame Schneider's pride and joy, her new Gaggia. This machine scared Kristina half to death with the high pressure hissing and spitting when she pulled the lever, but she was slowly getting the hang of it. The espresso was served with *schlagobers* and finely powdered sugar. She had barely placed the cup down when Bernhard appeared with a plate of steaming apricot pancakes. All was well in Cafe Braunerhof.

It was a busy Tuesday morning, but Kristina coped well. She had worked at the cafe since she had left school when she was fourteen. Herr Schneider had been fond of her and had forgiven many minor mishaps during her first year, but since his death, Madame Schneider had become short-tempered and demanding and Kristina was pleased when the young Bernhard had come to take over in the kitchen. He was as tall and stringy as a beanpole, but he had a radiant smile and always had a kind word. And he could bake like an angel.

Quickly, dish after exquisite dish had appeared out of the kitchen: *Linzertorte*; filbert slices; almond nut roulade; *punschkrapfen*; coffee rings and golden dumplings. Soon, Cafe Braunerhof had gained a good reputation and Madame Schneider was delighted to overhear a conversation in the market: '...and I have never tasted *apfelstrudel* as good in all my life! You must go there, my dear, it's all delicious!'

Soon, Madame Schneider was talking of taking on another girl to help serve the customers, and even wondering if she could squash another couple of tables in the corner. Every night she counted up the schillings in the till and every night there were more than the night before. Perhaps even Bernhard should have an assistant?

Kristina watched it all with great interest. These days, every night as she left for home, she was given a paper bag to take home to her family. It contained any left-over pasties and cakes, as only the freshest could be sold each day: they now had a reputation to keep up! And every night, Kristina would give a couple of the pastries to the poor old man who would sit on the pavement outside the cafe, begging, a few meagre coins lying on the pavement beside him.

'Bless you, my dear,' he would say gratefully. She learned that his name was Felix Koller and he had been injured in the recent war with Germany. He seemed very old indeed to Kristina and she worried for his welfare as she saw people stop at the window to gaze in at the wondrous display of delights, then pass by giving Felix not a thought.

One day, Kristina saw another, even older man stop at the window. He was gazing at the centrepiece: *Sachertorte*, with its carefully cut slice lying beside it. He was transfixed, and she was sure she saw him gulp, as if his mouth was watering. He stood for several minutes, looking at the cake from every angle, then, suddenly, put his hand in his pocket and pulled out some coins. He examined them very carefully for a minute, as if counting up every groschen, then handed the whole lot to Felix, as if defeated.

The poor man, thought Kristina, *he hasn't enough to pay for a slice himself, so he's given what he has to Felix! How kind he is.*

From then on, as the April blossom buds burst in the trees on the Herrengass, and the street was filled with the scents of cherry and almond blossom, the old man came to gaze in at the window of Cafe Braunerhof almost every day. He wore a heavy winter coat of good quality, but it hung loose on his sparse frame. Kristina thought it had probably once belonged to someone else. He wore a thick woollen scarf and a hat that had seen better days and Kristina wondered whether she should bring in a coat of her father's that might fit him better. He examined every item with great interest, but always went back to gaze at the *Sachertorte*, the flawless chocolate coating seeming to fascinate him. Most days, he counted up his groschen, pondered for a minute and then handed them to Felix.

Now, every day the shop was crowded as the reputation of Cafe Braunerhof grew. Many said that the pastrycook was as good as Georg, at the Cafe Demel, that he had an exceptional talent in one so young. Madame Schneider's mood improved as the schillings added up in the till and she took on a young girl called Hannah to help with the washing-up, the sweeping of floors and running the errands to the market. Bernhard chose a young boy to help in the kitchen, doing some of the jobs that Kristina had 'helped' with. She scarcely saw Bernhard in the shop these days, but then one day as they left in the evening, he shyly asked if he could walk her home. Her cheeks blushed as pink as the sky on a summer evening.

The following day, after the usual crush of customers at lunchtime, the old man arrived at his usual place at the window outside, but instead of standing quietly for a few minutes before he disappeared along the Herrengass, he opened the cafe door and walked in. Kristina made sure that he was seated comfortably at a table in the corner and asked him if he wanted to order something, deciding that if he hadn't enough money to pay for it, she would make it up from her own wages.

'I will have a slice of *Sachertorte*,' he said quietly, 'and an *Einspanner* coffee.'

Kristina took the finest porcelain plate and cut a large slice of *Sachertote*, put a generous helping of *schlagobers* on the side and took it to the old man. She poured a cup of their strongest, finest black coffee and delivered it to his table. He had picked up his silver fork, but sat looking at the cake, feasting with his eyes, marvelling at the perfect glossy sheen on the chocolate, the fine texture of the chocolate sponge, the layer of apricot, glistening so temptingly that his mouth watered, even though he had already dined on a fine lunch.

'Is everything to your satisfaction, Monsieur?' Kristina asked. He nodded. She was calculating the number of schillings she would have to put in the till if he couldn't pay. He finally took a piece of the gleaming chocolate onto his fork and tasted, closing his eyes in exquisite pleasure. How was it that the surface was so crisp, yet the moment he put it in his mouth it melted like snow on a hot summer's day? A morsel of sponge followed, as light as the feathers on a newly-hatched chick and the glistening apricot jam, well, there was a hint of something magical about it, but what? Slivovitz? Perhaps, but not quite. Without doubt it was the best *Sachertote* he had ever tasted! Soon every crumb on his plate had gone and he sat sipping his coffee, a rather grumpy expression on his face. Kristina was alarmed.

Madame Schneider's ample form came bustling into the front of the shop from her office. She took one look at the old man and sailed over to him like a galleon with a brisk following wind. 'Ah, Herr Gruber.' She said in her sweetest voice. 'What a *great* pleasure to see you here.' She eyed his empty plate. 'Would you like something else? *Linzertorte*, perhaps? A slice of *apfelstrudel*? Another coffee?'

'Another coffee, perhaps.'

Madame Schneider scuttled back to the counter where Kristina was standing, open-mouthed. 'Do you know him, Madame?' she whispered.

'Of course I know him,' she hissed. 'It's Jakob Gruber! He is the owner of the Cafe Demel, our greatest rivals!'

Kristina carried the coffee to his table and put it down, her hand suddenly trembling with nerves. He beckoned her close and whispered: 'Would you get that young man of yours, Bernhard, to come and have a talk with me later, at the Cafe Demel? I have a proposition to put to him...'

Alone

I am not lonely

JUST ALONE

Yes, just me

ON MY OWN

A silence seeps all around

Smothering each and every sound

That tries to trespass

on what I have found

I wait, patiently

As day turns to night

And night turns to day

The silence and shadows

drift slowly away

Another page turned

Another stepping stone

NO, I'm not lonely

JUST ALONE

WARREN DAVIES

The Long Road to Dathcreag.

JUDITH BARRIE

I've always wanted an old stone cottage of my own, and now I've got one. I wonder how long it will be before the novelty wears off, before the picturesque becomes a nuisance? Before the drip into the bedroom from the roof becomes beyond enduring, or the door, so tight in its frame to begin with, refuses to open one damp winter morning and I am entombed. Just a pile of bones to be found mouldering in a corner, years from now.

I've decided to keep a diary – I'm supposed to be here writing, anyway. That's what I told the boatman, when he brought me over.

"And what will a wee lassie like you be doing on that godforsaken island?"

"I'm a writer," I told him. (As if!) And that my name was Laura Mackenzie, I'd never liked Jennifer. Or Brady.

Thursday, 20th April.

Did loads of shopping in Tobermory – it was like being on Desert Island Discs, I could only carry ten CDs, this time, so I had to choose my favourites. Rachmaninov figured prominently and Ravel, with a compilation of George Michael thrown in. Loads of batteries, of course. And tons of food. Duncan, my very friendly boatman had already ferried across the bulk of my gear earlier in the day. He'll be calling every Wednesday at ten, to take me over to Tobermory and bring me back at three. Slept like a log.

I'd been lucky with the boat trip across – *Don't expect this every week*, Duncan had told me. *You can get fair drookit in the winter!* (I am learning this language word by word. Drookit – soaked to the skin.) But I don't care about the winter, that's months ahead and just now I'm in a state of euphoria enjoying my freedom. The sense of relief and release is overwhelming, a bit like being tipsy. I am wandering round the cliff-top 'garden' grinning at seabirds, shouting into the wind – *You can't get at me now, Steven Brady, you can't touch me now*!

Friday 21st April.

Not sure if I'll have time to do this diary – I'm too busy! Spent nearly all day walking and exploring. A glass of malt and to bed with the gloaming, my new routine.

I was up with the sunshine and set out to explore. I was able to walk the whole perimeter of the island in just over two hours, and that was sauntering, trying to take it all in. I passed the other cottage, deserted, of course, and was back 'home' by lunch. Although there's no fridge, there's a small larder with an open metal grille facing north and it had kept things surprisingly cool. I had cheese and tomatoes on fresh, crusty bread – that won't last long.

And all this had been arranged by my dear friend, Mark.

I'd first met Mark twenty years ago, when he was in his early twenties and I was coming up to forty. He was running a small fancy goods shop on the High Street and when I went in to look at a small clock I'd seen in the window, he'd put his book down to serve me: he was reading *Bleak House* by Charles Dickens, one of my favourites. I ended up chatting with him for nearly an hour and after that we spent a lot of time together, eventually forming our own book club, just the two of us, and he would come round to discuss his latest read. We adored each other in our innocent way but it wasn't long after that I met Steve and Mark met Ronnie. It would be fair to say that we were both utterly smitten.

Ronnie was already big in the music business and had easily made his first million, managing groups like Purple Phantom and Peach Kaleidoscope. After 'courting' for a couple of months, Mark moved in with him and they have stayed together happily ever since.

Steve wasn't keen that I had a male friend. '*But he's gay!*' I reasoned, '*I'm old enough to be his mother!*' But Steve wouldn't budge on the matter – he 'loved me so much that he wanted me all to himself,' and fortunately (for him) Mark and Ronnie moved to L.A shortly after and I didn't see Mark again for almost another twenty years.

Tonight, when I was getting undressed for bed, I plucked up courage and looked in the mirror. The bruises were as spectacular as the sunset had been half an hour before, but a lot more tender.

Saturday 22nd April.

> *Scudding clouds tearing in from the west and a sprinkle*
> *of raindrops – but not enough to get 'drookit'. Climbed*
> *down the cliff – to look at the pebbles on the beach. High*
> *tide at noon. Sleeping better than I have done for years.*

Climbing down the cliff was a lot easier than it sounds; it's only about twenty feet down to the wide strip of large pebbles, with plenty of footholds on the way. I felt like a child again mooching about in rock pools, collecting bladderwrack with the ambitious idea of drying it out to burn on the fire. Although every day had been warmer than the one before, I was, after all, planning on a long stay.

The cottage was beautifully kitted out with every luxury as befits a millionaire – except for electricity! The water gurgled thirty yards from the door, crystal clear, freezing cold, with a taste a very long way from what came out of the taps in Ilford. Apparently, Ronnie and Mark had spent a lot of time up here in the early days, when Ronnie first bought the island and they made sure they had (almost) every comfort.

It had been quite a shock when I bumped into Mark on a trip into London, a couple of months ago. We fell into each other's arms, dived into the nearest Costa and spent the next two hours 'catching up'. It was a particularly bad time for me. Over the previous months Steve's violent episodes had become more and more frequent as his drinking had spiralled out of control. He'd been having an affair with a woman at work, I told Mark, and when she ended it he went completely off the rails, lashing out at me. I rolled up my sleeves and showed him the bruises on my arms – Steve always hurt me where it wouldn't show. The tears had welled up and Mark was horrified: *Leave him! Just put your clothes in a case and just leave him! I'll make sure you're okay! I'll look after you!*

I'd explained that it wasn't so simple. Steve didn't want me, but he didn't want anyone else to have me. He needed someone to punish, and that was *me*. I didn't tell Mark that it had been going on for years, almost from the beginning; that I'd been a bloody fool for putting up with it, because I was too ashamed to admit it to anybody.

Ronnie was away filming in South America for a few weeks so after that, I met up with Mark regularly, and Steve never found out - well, not until *that* night.

Sunday, 23rd April.

Very windy today so spent the morning looking through the five shelves of books in the back room. Most are much as to be expected: Wilbur Smith, Lee Child, Tom Clancy, but – and here is Mark's touch – a full maroon leather-bound set of Dickens! If ever I get chance to read them.

The cottage has a large kitchen with flagged stone floor and a huge stone sink. There is a stove, of sorts, but that requires burning wood from the lean-to at the side of the cottage. The wooden table is so substantial that, sail attached, you could set out to sea on it. There are four assorted wooden chairs, and a well-seasoned rocking chair, replete with a dozen cushions, in front of the fireplace. Any hot water comes from a boiler at the back of the fire. I suppose in the hot weather I could bathe in the sea, an interesting thought.

There is the 'back room' with two decent leather sofas and a large cupboard as well as the bookshelves; a miniature bathroom, of the more primitive kind, and a bedroom upstairs, with a large double bed and posh linen, which was only slightly damp when I arrived.

Outside, the lean-to houses all manner of goodies. Besides the neatly stacked piles of firewood, I have a ladder, spade and various other tools and implements and a couple of wicker baskets, which I can take out to collect driftwood and seaweed.

I would never have had the courage to do what I did without Mark's help. Steve was so vicious and vindictive that I would have to disappear, completely. I couldn't just leave him, like a normal person. He would have searched me out and dragged me back, beating me into submission in the process. Ronnie, on the other hand, would give Mark anything he wanted without a murmur, so had had no hesitation when Mark asked him if I could stay on Dathcreag – for a year. Or two. *No problem, Sweetheart*, he had said to Mark, *Whatever makes you happy*.

I'm glad one of us found happiness.

Monday, 24th April.

Spent most of the day walking round the island again. Saw a small herd of horned wild goats. I have a great view of Mull from the east side of the island – looking forward to Wednesday when I can get over there again. Getting the hang of the stove and heated some soup for lunch, followed by rice pudding and coffee.

The weather was glorious this morning, with a gentle breeze – it's always windy, right up to storm force, so 'gentle breeze' is as good as it gets. So I trotted off, basket on arm for another circuit of the island. I have a good view of Mull on the east side, so that I can easily make out the colourful sea-front shops at Ballygown. The sea was calm, the bees were buzzing in the gorse hedges and I felt happier than I had ever done in my entire life. Suddenly I came across eight wild goats, lazily munching at the bushes and pulling at the long grass, liberally peppered with dozens of wildflowers. The primroses were scattered everywhere and clumps of thrift clung to every rocky outcrop. The goats showed not the slightest alarm but stared at me with their curious letter-box eyes as I picked my way along the path, never pausing in the serious business of chewing. Mark told me that many times they'd seen seals and dolphins, but never an eagle. But there was a whole host of seabirds: puffins, kittiwakes and razor bills, guillemots and stormy petrels. They kept a lovely reference book in the cottage that would help me identify them.

Tuesday, 25th April.

Looking forward to my trip to Mull tomorrow, I have my shopping list ready. Heated enough water to do a bit of washing, which I pegged out on the line across the garden, amazed that it dried in half an hour with the stiff sea breeze and sunshine. Went down the cliff and gathered seaweed –

the first lot is drying out nicely – and some unusual shells.
Small crabs in the rock pools.

I love this place. Why on earth did I ever put up with Steve for all that miserable time? Nearly twenty years of my life, wasted, afraid to say something out of place, afraid to speak to other people, afraid of life. He once put his hands around my throat and almost choked me – because I wasn't smiling! What did I ever have to smile about?

And now, I walk around with a permanent grin on my face. Mark will look after me. When I phoned him, that awful night, he came straight round, helped me pack a few things and whisked me off to safety. Steve had been looking at my mobile and demanded to know who this 'Mark' was, this man I'd been phoning for the last three months. I told him he was a gay friend, married to Ronnie Beckinsale, the famous music producer, but it made no difference. He hit me so hard across the face that I fell to the floor. And then he started to kick me, repeatedly, taking pleasure in my pleading sobs. He probably broke a couple of my ribs, but I knew they would mend, in time, like my broken heart.

Wednesday, 26th April.

Duncan appeared on the dot of ten and rowed me over to Mull. Calm seas and a gentle breeze. I wandered round the town with not a care in the world – it's a long way from Ilford. Had a coffee and a sticky bun in a lovely teashop, bought some more CDs (Barbara Streisand and Puccini) and loads of provisions from the Co-op store. I picked up my mail from the post office.

There was only one letter and that was from Mark. Usually, Duncan, the boatman, never stops talking for a minute, so I saved it until I got back to the cottage to read it in peace. There was a bit of chatty news: Ronnie was home and they were going to Tuscany for a few weeks R & R. He had enclosed a cutting from the Ilford Gazette: the police have found Steve's body – with over twenty stab wounds! God! Did I really do that many? - And they are looking for a Mrs Jennifer Brady in connection with the crime. Good luck with that!

I unpacked all the shopping and put the Barbara Streisand CD on the player: *New York State of Mind*, belting it out at full volume to the seagulls, singing along with the words. Then I made a lovely meal of fresh haddock, new potatoes and peas

102

Brittle Bones

Lithe and lissom
These limbs once young
Now they creak
On every rung.

Each step I take
I leave behind
My distant youth
I cannot find.

My head is bowed
My back is bent
The borrowed years
Are all but spent.

For these brittle bones
Which curse the cold
There is no fun
In growing old.

WARREN DAVIES

The Orphan

VERONICA SCOTTON

She found a diamond bracelet in the back of a car and slipped it into her pocket before he saw it.

Life hadn't always been like this. Only a few months ago, she had lived in a roomy apartment with her parents and 3 brothers. She remembered helping her mother to cook and serve dinner in the evening, always thanking God for the food, before eating and then enjoying the lively conversation around the dining table. As the youngest child, and only daughter, she had been expected to help her mother with the housework, but she was also spoiled by her brothers and father. Hardly a week would go by without her father bringing her a new book, or a small piece of jewelry. Her brothers would bring her sweets or little toys. They would tease her and tell her stories, always bringing a smile to her face. One day her brother Hamsah brought her a kitten, she named it Kitkat and showered it with affection, taking it to visit her grandparents who also lived in the apartments. The family was very close.

That life had come to a devastating end, just as the weather was becoming warmer. Coming back from school, she stopped to listen to a blind beggar playing a flute. His music was enchanting and she would have tossed a coin into the hat at his feet, if she had had any. Instead, she went into a nearby market stall, the vendor was a friend of her father, and she often played with his daughter. "Could I have one of your kebabs, Mr Alkarma, I will bring you the money at the weekend, when I receive my spends". Mahdi Alkarma had a soft spot for this little girl, and he had seen her watching the beggar. He said, "Take the food, Danyah, you don't need to repay me, poor Jamal lost his family and his sight last summer during the fighting with the Syrian Armed Forces and Salafi jihadist groups.

She gave the kebab to Jamal, and stopped to chat, telling him how much she loved his music, but suddenly he grabbed her arm and shouted, "Run away, I hear planes, get away from buildings".

She ran into a nearby orange grove with Jamal running beside her. He pushed her to the ground and lay on top of her, just as the planes began to drop their deadly cargo. She lay there, pinned down by the beggar for what seemed like hours. As the noise of the bombardment faded away, she crawled from under the Jamal's lifeless body, and stretched her cramped muscles. In the gloom of the smoky, dusty air, Danyah looked around at the carnage surrounding her, it was difficult to get her bearings. Not only was the air thick with dust, and tall buildings flattened, but also the sounds of the evening had changed. Gone was the chatter of old men sitting outside of their homes, drinking tea and arguing about football. The usual sound of music coming through open windows was replaced by frantic families, tearing at the rubble with their hands calling out, for loved ones.

Danyah found her way to the apartments in which she had lived, there were a few people with torches, they were whispering to one another and listening for sounds of life. She heard them talking "Not much chance of survivors here, this building took a direct hit". As she stared around, one of the flashlights illuminated something familiar, she crawled over the derelict building until she found what had caught her eye, the beautiful unique carpet, that her mother had designed. The whole family, under her instruction had helped to weave the intricate patterns, and it had taken nearly two years to finish. It would have become a family heirloom. A voice in the darkness rang out, "Get away from here little girl, this isn't a playground, it's not safe to play here." She didn't cry, she was cold and shaking, she walked away stunned.

She carried on walking along the road, away from the destruction, until she dropped with exhaustion, then crawled into long grass to sleep.

The next morning, Danyah awoke. Her mouth was dry, her stomach griping. She got to her feet and continued walking until she came to a farm, on the edge of a village. A dog barking and other early morning animal noises could be heard nearby. She spotted a water pump and helped herself to a drink.

A voice called out, "Hey you, what are you doing, get off this land, it's private" She didn't stop, but continued to pump the water, catching it in her mouth. The boy behind the voice ran towards her and pushed her over.

"I said get away, tramp" She was not used to being spoken to like that and shouted back at him. "What's your problem, can't you spare a drop of water?"

"Not for the likes of you we can't."

"The likes of me?, I'll have you know my father is a doctor, my brother is at university…" Her voice faded away, as the memory of the day before hit her. She had no father, mother or brothers. She had no home, or grandparents, or kitten. Her shoulders began to shake, the tears ran down her cheeks. She related the events of the last 24 hours to the boy, shouting and crying as the mixed emotions of anger, grief and fear fought for domination within her.

The boy looked at her afresh. If she wasn't telling the truth, she was a very good actor and beneath the dirt, was a well-dressed girl. Perhaps he could make use of her. His body language towards her softened and he listened to her with fake sympathy, but she didn't trust him. "Come with me," he said, "I have friends who could help you." She hesitated, but what choice did she have! "Come on, you can trust me, I swear on my mother's grave." He looked the kind to swear on anything. Her family had warned her about boys like him.

Hesitantly, she followed him into the farmhouse, where a man and a woman sat eating breakfast. "Make room for a guest," he said and introduced the couple as Omar and Sidrah. The three people started talking very quickly, they had a strange dialect that she struggled to understand, but she got the impression that the boy was relating her story of the bombing and about having no-one to turn to. They didn't speak directly to her but gave her a plate with flat bread and hummus and she ate hungrily, as she tried to understand what they were saying.

The woman turned towards her and spoke softly, she led her into a bathroom and gave her clean clothes to change into. Perhaps these people could help her after all. She bathed and dressed and brushed her long dark hair. The woman took her clothes away to wash them, and in the evening, they once again shared their meal with her. They gave her a mat to sleep on, and a blanket to cover herself. The next morning the boy and the man went out, she guessed, to work on the farm, the woman busied herself around the house. In the evening they invited her once more to share their food and indicated that she could sleep there once more.

After breakfast on the second day, Danya dressed in her own clothes which the woman had washed and ironed. The boy told her to get into the car and Omar would take her to friends who could help her. He said that they worked for a charity who would make enquiries into the bombings, to ascertain if any of her family had survived. She eagerly climbed into the passenger seat and smiled in gratitude at the man.

An hour later, the car pulled up outside a large house, Omar got out, indicating for her to stay where she was. She watched him talking to another scruffy looking man, dressed in stained overalls, who looked over to where she was sitting. Money changed hands and then Omar shouted for her to come out of the car. She got out and walked slowly towards the house. He walked back to the car, without saying a word and stuffed the money into his pocket. He drove off without a backward glance. This didn't feel right, she stood nervously looking at this other man as he looked her up and down. He asked her how old she was and she answered that she was ten. "That'll do," he said mysteriously. He took her into the house and pointed to the kitchen sink which was piled high with dirty dishes. "There's the stove, there's the kettle, I've got a business to run, I want this place clean and a meal on the table before I return at 6 o'clock." He locked the door on his way out. She had been sold as a slave.

Danyah cried with terror and grief as she cleaned the filthy house. She had no idea where she was. At 5 o'clock she looked into the cupboards and found rice and vegetables and made a risotto. The following day she learned that the man's name was Moutaz and that he sold secondhand cars and ran a car repair shop. After a few days, when the level of cleanliness in the house was acceptable to him, he took her to the garage, and set her to work, cleaning the interiors of the cars, after he had finished repairing them. He instructing her to hand over to him, anything of value that she found. Over the years he had been pleasantly surprised at the things the owners mislaid inside secondhand cars. The clients were pleased at this extra service, getting their cars returned to them shining clean and often tipped Moutaz. This girl was worth the money he had paid for her.

One evening as she was clearing up the dishes from the evening meal, he beckoned her towards him. He grabbed her hand and pulled her to sit on his knee. She was very innocent, but this didn't feel right, she jumped up and pulled away from him. He laughed at her, "OK then, not tonight, I'm tired anyway, but there will be changes."

The next day as she wracked her brain to think of a way to escape, he sent her to clean another car. "Make a good job of this one, he's a good customer." It was, as she cleaned out the back of the car, that she spotted something shining, in-between the seats. Her slim fingers soon retrieved the beautiful, diamond bracelet. She would hide it with the cache of coins that she had found over the course of the last few weeks.

Over time, Moutaz stopped bothering to lock the door when he left her in the house. He had started to give her money to do the shopping or run other errands. He no longer worried about her running away. Where would she go? On one of these shopping trips, Danyah decided to go into a cafe to shelter from the heat of the day, she handed over a couple of coins in exchange for a chilled drink. The shopping bags were heavy and she was glad to rest them on the floor, while the cool liquid wet her dry dusty throat.

As she glanced around the cafe, she noticed a young man writing, and was puzzled to see that he was using both hands. He seemed to be writing something on his left side, with his left hand and then using his right hand to write something on another paper. She was so riveted on this strange behaviour, that she didn't notice that he had glanced towards her. He put the pen down and she looked at his face without any shyness. He smiled at her and said "Hello" then introduced himself politely as Asif. He said, 'I saw you watching me, are you surprised that I can use both hands to write with?" She smiled back and nodded. He went on, "More people would be able to do it if children weren't forced to use the predominant hand only. Have you heard of Leonardo Da Vinci? He famously could use both hands to write and draw. Come here and have a go." Intrigued she walked over to his table. He gave her a clean sheet of paper and she tried to write with her left hand, with disastrous results, then laughed at her efforts. The young man laughed with her. It seemed a very long time since anyone had made her laugh or even spoken kindly to her. She asked him what he was doing and he answered, "Can you keep a secret?" She nodded. "My handwriting is different, when I use my left hand, so I can sign my name as a different person." She had no idea why anyone would want to do that, so she presumed that he was teasing her, as her brothers often had, and she laughed at him. She found herself relaxing and slowly she began to tell him about working in the garage. He listened so sincerely that she found herself telling him everything, from the beggar to the bracelet.

The kindly young man told her that he would help her. He said that he came to the cafe at the same time every week. If she ever found herself free at this time, to come and meet him and he would see what he could do. The next week, Moutaz was in a foul mood, he shouted and slapped her for not preparing his favourite meal properly, and for fighting off his advances. He locked her in the house and didn't come back for two days. The following week she was working in the garage, when he told her to clean out a car and then sweep the floor. Then he went out. He had never left her alone in the garage before, she decided to take a chance and go to the cafe. She took her little cache of coins and the bracelet and ran all the way, deciding that if the man could just find her somewhere else to live she might never need to see the abusive car mechanic again.

When she reached the cafe, the young man was there, his smile for her lit up his face, and he came towards her and enveloped her in a hug. The physical contact felt good and she felt herself relaxing into his embrace. He said, "I'm so glad you could get away, I think I can help you. There is transport arranged to take a family to France, you could travel with them. A child alone in France will be put into foster care. You will be able to go to school, you will be safe'. She was shocked, she hadn't considered that she would be going abroad, but the man persuaded her that it was a good opportunity, as Syria, in these troubled times, was not a safe place for an orphan child. She found herself being persuaded. She handed over the bracelet to him as he led her to his car and took her to meet the family. That night she stayed with the couple and their two young children. She felt so relaxed in their company that all her fears melted away, and she began to look forward to this new adventure. In the early hours of the morning, before the sun had had a chance to warm the air, she was woken, given a warm coat and told to move quietly and quickly. She followed the couple and climbed into a lorry, which surprisingly was already more than half full of people. The engine kept running as they climbed aboard and pulled away before they had time to make themselves comfortable.

An hour later, the lorry stopped to pick up more travellers, now they were very cramped and several people were complaining, saying how many thousands of Syrian pounds they had paid for this journey and that they had expected more suitable transport. Danyah thought about the bracelet that she had handed over and gave silent thanks to the generous man for not asking her for more money.

The lorry travelled for two days, stopping only occasionally to enable people to relieve themselves behind bushes. They had all brought food and drink with them which some of them generously shared with her. She was very grateful and repaid them by entertaining the children on board, getting them to sing songs or play games to relieve the boredom. Dusk was falling as the lorry stopped on the outskirts of Calais. The couple and their young children had become close to the girl and were disinclined to leave her alone in a foreign country, they asked her if she wanted to travel with them. They had family in England and a cousin had arranged for them to travel over the Chanel. They had contacted their English relatives who were willing to welcome an extra child.

It was 2 a.m. when the family received a call to say that the cousin had landed in Calais and was on his way to pick them up. They were exhausted by the time a tiny car pulled up and they all squashed into the back. Keeping to the back streets, they soon reached a tiny cove and saw the little fishing boat. They were told to board as quickly as possible, hide under fishing nets and stay there until they were out to sea. 15 minutes later with tiredness forgotten, the family and crew celebrated the last leg of their escape.

Danyah looked up at the millions of stars in the sky and relaxed for the first time in months. She fell into a deep, dreamless sleep.

Her slumber was shattered by the noise of terrified screaming. The pilot did everything in his power to make the boat go faster and to steer it away from danger. As the cruise liner bore down upon them, her last thought was of the handsome young man and the way he wrote with both hands.

Cue Music

"Listen with Mother" at quarter to two,
"Woman's Hour" at two o'clock,
Then "Mrs Dale" at four fifteen,
The tunes told us the times.

"Children's Hour" with Uncle Mac
Playing Larry the Lamb in Toytown,
Wandering with Nomad, Jennings at School,
Then "Goodnight children, everywhere."

The excitement as "The Devil's Gallop"
Brought Dick Barton, with Snowy and Jock.
But they pulled the plug for homework's sake
And "The Archers" came and took its place.
The pictures we saw were better by far
Than those on the new silver screens.
And there they remain, forgotten until
The music revives them again.

BARBARA SHEARWOOD

Murder in the Mansion

COLIN BALMER

'Or else…' was enough of a threat to ensure our Nipper's silence. My little brother would not tell anyone what we had found or done. He would agree to anything to protect his privileged place with our gang (although Mam's insistence that I look after him meant he would always be my albatross). So it was that on the day we ventured further afield, his reticence was assured.

But I'm getting in front of myself. In the early fifties. we were living at my maternal grandparents with two of my uncles in a dilapidated three-storey terraced house in Ardwick. The area would, on reflection, have been classified a slum by today's standards, but to us it was simply a home. Our playground was the inner-city bomb-ravaged streets. We had dens and forts and ships and castles in the precarious masonry of buildings guarded by railings and **Danger Keep Out** signs. Neither was an adequate defence against curious 10–12-year-old boys, even with a junior sibling in tow. Jimmy, Ecker, Tommy and up to a half dozen other youngsters, usually led by *Alby the Bold,* made up our Palmerston Street gang. We fought with and against a comprehensive array of Indians, Gerries, Japs and pirates during the long summer holidays in the streets around Ancoats Hospital. Our fortresses, galleons, castles and dens were built in the debris of both the recent war and aggressive council rehousing to the suburbs. Ecker was a particularly good den builder, who aspired to become a brickie when he grew up.

As fashions change so do the imaginary foes shown in the latest matinee films and widely circulated American comics. Ecker, Alby and me, with Nipper tagging along, took up the challenge of rooting out spies as the American inspired paranoia targeted the commie threat. The transition to a less physical conflict frustrated powerful Peter Eckershalgh. He was as big as someone two years older. if you wanted someone on your side in a fight, you couldn't better 'Ecker.' But this day would not include any major battles. Commie spies were devious and cowardly, would not face you man to man and were likely to stab you in the back when you weren't looking – and they employed girls!

We had ventured about a dozen streets from our own territory when we came across the likely HQ of a red cluster in an abandoned Victorian monolith ostentatiously named Trefoil House and protected by a seven-foot-high wall and **Danger Keep Out** signs. After skirting the wall, we came upon a conveniently fallen tree at the rear of the house. This gave an easy climb onto the wall, from which we dropped, demonstrating the perfect paratroopers' roll on landing. Our kid managed to scrawp his knees after a clumsy landing and tripping over an unrestrained shoelace. Spit and hanky doctored the wound and we moved on.

Collecting broken branches to fabricate ordnance on the way, we kept under cover in the rhododendron thicket. We leapfrogged each other – the vanguard to plot our further progress, the rear guard to watch for pursuers as we reached the house safely. We found a unboarded window through which we posted Nipper, being the smallest and lightest. He quickly found an unlocked door and let us in.

Once inside, we found ourselves in what must have been the kitchen, the room was bare of all furnishings and equipment. Gas and electricity had long since been disconnected. A copy of the Evening Chron lay on the floor. Was the ringed entry a secret commie message? I read it to my troop 'Vodka Martini - 2:30 at Newark.' We needed the code book but found nothing in the kitchen. We were further disappointed that no knives or even skewers had been left behind – Alby wanted a meat cleaver. What could we do if we came up against a foreign spy?

A deep layer of dust covered every surface, flypapers splattered with dry cadavers hung from the whitewashed ceiling, gloomy light crept past the window boards. We felt a coldness that could not be assigned to the air temperature. A noise from somewhere below in the cellar startled us and urged us into the squashed sardine safety of a narrow pantry before exhaling in unison and relief. Nipper hugged my waist, trembling as silence returned.

A spy! – the common thought invaded our minds separately.

Alby proposed, 'Naw, 'sprobbly only a rat. We 'ave 'em at 'ome.'

'Oh, we ain't scared of no rats?' offered Ecker with less than comforting bravado and a glance round for reassurance.

'Nah,' said I with thumbs in my waistband in my best Jimmy Cagney, 'Come out you doidy rat and get what's cummin' to you.'

I pointed my sycamore sourced six-gun at the door and **Bang! Bang! Bang!** released the tension.

Then we set out exploring further. The bone-dry dust on the hitherto polished wooden floor of the large drawing room made a good rink in the absence of frozen pond. All the other rooms downstairs were similarly bare and dust covered, wallpaper peeled from all surfaces, not a pane of glass intact, not a splinter of furniture - all the signs of desertion and neglect apart from a single flat bottle on by the front door. The bottle, which you might say was spade shaped, had a strangely familiar Christmassy smell – Alby guessed it might have held poison or drugs. We had to investigate further.

The stairs were broken in places and every other step was missing, the banister was rickety, missing nearly half the spindles and hanging at a precarious angle. Alby declared the stairs 'dangerous', but we ventured onwards and upwards regardless with childish confidence. We weren't heavy enough to fall through anyway and were putting distance between us and the rats in the cellar at the same time.

We gained the landing and saw four rooms off and a further flight of stairs, which we could investigate later. I thought I got a hint of my uncles' Saturday night smell – you know the beer and cigarettes stink they bring back from the pub. The smell got stronger as Alby opened the door to the second bedroom. The three of us and Nipper piled into the room and stopped, rooted to the spot at the sight that met us as the door swung closed. No one expected to come across a body in a deserted house. Spreadeagled on the floor was a man showing no signs of life.

With the astute wisdom of a kid, our Nipper said, 'It's a body!'

'Do you think he's dead?' asked Ecker.

I knew what I was looking at. 'Yes. He's been murdered.'

'How do you know he's been murdered?'

'You can always tell. When the detectives get to a murder, they always chalk a line round the corpse, so if someone moves it again, they know how he died and where.'

'So what?' challenged Alby.

Ironic that it is me, 'Barmy Balmer', who explains it to the unenlightened pals.

'The shape they draw is like this. He is face down. His arms are spread out - like he's flying and his legs are bent like he's running. Look at the body on the floor – it's exactly like the chalk drawings they do of the bodies in the murder films.'

They agree with my analysis and speculate.

'I bet he's one of them anarkicks and our secret agents have bumped him off.'

114

'Or it might be a Rusky who got uncovered by MI5 and eliminated.'

'Or maybe a conshy or deserter from the war…'

Nipper brought us back to earth, 'I'm gonna tell my Mam. And you'll get done for goin' in bombed houses. And she'll tell the police. And they will put you all in prison.'

'Shurrup Nip. You say nowt, or else…'

He complied with my order.

Ecker said what we all felt, 'Let's get out of here. If anyone finds us they'll think we murdered him.'

We left the building observing the gang rules of stealth as we retraced our steps.

When we reached the garden, a movement in the bushes attracted Ecker's eye.

'I bet that rat's in there,' he said picking up a stone.

We joined in the stoning of the bush and were surprised when a rabbit jumped out. This demanded our immediate attention and had to be chased. We gave up when it vanished though a hole in the wall.

During our walk home we pledged to say nothing to anyone about the murder in case first, we were accused or second, the murderer would come after us as witnesses and kill us – or third and crucially, we would get in serious trouble.

I don't think any of us slept soundly that night, other than my younger brother of course, who wasn't old enough to understand what had been going on.

The following day, our adventures took us down to the canal, fishing with jam jars and throwing stones. Anne Fingy, a good fighter and goalkeeper – conferred with an honorary widgy - therefore a virtual boy, Jimmy Partridge and Olly Longshaw were all along with us. We stuck to our pact and the murder in the mansion was not mentioned. But I couldn't wait to report back to the gang what I learned at teatime that evening.

Over the tater 'ash, Uncle John asked Uncle Pete if he'd heard about old Ernie Hardwick.

'No. I've not seen him for a day or two. What's the old drunk up to now?'

'It seems he had one over the eight the other night and got lost on his way home.'

'Nowt new there is there?'

'Yes, he broke into one of those boarded up big houses to sleep it off. It seems the police saw the door open and found him unconscious upstairs. They took him back to the station for questioning about his so-called accomplices. They think he's some kind of Fagin character, using kids to do his dirty work.'

'Why would they think that?' I interrupted as my brother started to say, 'We saw a ...'

Uncle John explained, 'The police think he was using small kids to break in and rob houses around here. They say that loads of small footprints - like kids' size eleven or twelve and some even smaller – small footprints in the dust all around where they found Ernie. The police said the gang would be easy to trace and identify by their shoe sizes.'

'I see,' said I, 'He would be like in Oliver Twist what Miss Watson was telling my class about in school. Fagin was an evil man.'

My Uncle shook his head, 'He denied any knowledge of working with kids but couldn't explain away the hundreds of fresh small footprints in the dust.'

The conversation between my uncles then drifted into funny reminiscences about their own adventures growing up. I think they were putting it on for me and my brother when they romanced about '...climbing chimbleys, working down t'Bradford pit and trudging frew snow wivout no shoes on.'

I went to bed that night with my mind in turmoil. Tomorrow I would tell the gang how my detective skills had discovered the proper provenance of the body in the big house.

Most importantly, they must get their mams to buy new shoes and dump the incriminating footwear.

Stepping Stones

A Stepping Stone
That's what you are
Large or small Near or far.

I am here today But not tomorrow
Through life I plough A lonely furrow.

I'll say hello I'll say goodbye
Then move on Before you try.

To get too close And keep in touch
I enjoyed our time Thank you so much.

So! Please Try to understand
When I withdraw My heart and hand.

I won't look back Or write or telephone
After all, you are
A Stepping Stone.

WARREN DAVIES

Benches

DAVID LOCKLEY

Dylan Lunn shuffled out of his third charity shop of the day. He hadn't bought much. Just a couple of Star Trek DVDs and a t-shirt with a picture of an alien on it. Size XL.

He didn't usually bother looking at the clothing section. He had never taken much pride in his appearance and a lifetime of schoolyard taunts about his size had not helped to instil any sense of pride or self-esteem. 'Dylan Lunn, he weighs a ton' had been the mantra that had followed him throughout his school years. Then, as the teenage years unfolded before him like a bumpy rock-strewn road, his bad skin, wiry curly hair and unflattering spectacles had further coloured his relationship with the world around him and the people he felt so apart from.

He had liked the picture of the alien though.

He sauntered along the covered shopping precinct and tried to think of other shops he could visit, other places he could spend his time. The alternative was just going back home and that prospect didn't fill him with much joy. He lived with his mother and, though they got on passably well, the bleak shadowy confines of the house just served to remind him that, at 21 years old, he was doing very little with his life and, when all was said and done, he was still living with his mother.

The precinct was quiet today. A few people were sat in the small cafe but otherwise it was fairly deserted. He went past the manicurist, then the invisible menders ('that's a lie', he thought to himself, 'I can quite clearly see them') and then across the concourse near the Kindred Spirit shop, which sold what Dylan thought of as 'hippy nonsense, catering for all of your crystal dolphin and hemp dreamcatcher needs.' The smell of incense and scented candles coming out of the open doorway was quite pleasant though.

And, once again, he saw the man.

A few months earlier, the precinct management, or the council, or whoever, had set up some benches just outside the hippy shop with a sign on an easel. The sign read 'Chatty Benches. We welcome you to sit here to connect with others. Nobody needs to feel lonely in your community'. There were a few smiley emoji icons surrounding the words, trying their best to emphasise the positivity of the message.

Dylan thought it was a naive gesture. His disdain was not dimmed by the fact that he had only ever seen one person sat there. A single, elderly gentleman. White hair, shabby black coat and a sad, empty expression. It seemed ironic to Dylan that an initiative designed to bring people together was just serving to throw a spotlight on this guy's loneliness.

And here he was again, looking like he had just stepped out of a Lowry painting and plonked himself down on a bench.

Dylan was just about to wander past him, as he had done so many times before, but then, some tiny part of his mind flared like a match flame and convinced him to undermine the tragic irony of the situation. He walked over and, after a hesitant moment, he sat down next to the man. 'Hello.' he said.

The man had been staring into the middle distance, his face a mask of impassivity. But when he heard Dylan's voice, a light seemed to flicker into life in his surprisingly blue eyes and his whole expression brightened. Dylan couldn't help but think of the sun appearing from behind dark clouds.

'Hello,' replied the man, 'what's your name?' A gentle smile played upon the man's lips and crinkled the lines around his eyes.

'Dylan.'

'Hmm, interesting. Named after Dylan Thomas? Or Bob Dylan?'

'Well, my dad left behind a load of old rock records before he scarpered. Stones, Hendrix, that sort of thing.' replied Dylan, 'I think there are some Bob Dylan albums in there so probably him.'

The man nodded sagely, as if some great understanding had been imparted.

'So', he said, 'no dad, eh? That must be tough on you. Did he leave recently?'

Dylan suddenly realised that he was talking to this complete stranger as if he had known him for years and yet, it didn't seem strange or uncomfortable.

'No,' he replied, 'it was when I was very young. I barely remember him. It's just been me and mum for, well, for my whole life really.'

'No wife or girlfriend?' asked the man. 'Or boyfriend? One shouldn't make assumptions, I suppose.'

Dylan snorted with the derisory air of one who has known rejection intimately. In fact, the only intimacy he had ever known.

'No,' he replied, 'nobody. Just me and mum,'

'Take heart, young fellow,' replied the man, 'I am sure somebody special is out there somewhere, waiting for you. The Universe can sometimes take pity on the lonely and weave a couple of threads together in life's tapestry.'

'Do you really think so?' asked Dylan. 'I'm not so sure.'

The man's smile widened. 'Well, it's not an exact science but hope springs eternal. One must never give up hope, you know. Hope is like the stars that the ancient sailors used to navigate by. Keep your eye on hope and it will guide you to safe harbour and happy lands.'

There was something in the man's tone and comforting manner that cut through Dylan's usual surly cynicism and seemed to ignite a tiny light in the dark cavern of his heart. Looking into the man's eyes, he felt as if there might be some truth to his words, that there might actually be some sunny days after all, when all he had ever visualised before was an endless, rainy Tuesday, every day, for ever more.

'It is very good of you to sit and chat with me,' said the man, 'not everybody would take the time or be so considerate.'

'Yeah, well, that's ok. I'm not sure what made me sit down,' replied Dylan, 'to be honest I'd seen you a few times but today, I dunno, I just thought I would stop and have a chat.'

'And that's just what these benches are for, I suppose,' replied the man, 'it's good to chat. Talking to a stranger is like one soul acknowledging the presence of another soul. Don't you think so?'

Dylan shrugged and said, 'I guess so. I hadn't thought about it like that before.'

And, in truth, he hadn't. But talking to the man (whose name it hadn't even occurred to him to ask) felt like the most natural thing in the world. He felt lighter than he had for, well, than ever.

And so they talked. The sad, empty precinct seemed to disappear around them as they conversed on so many topics, on love, on family, on dreams and on aspirations, on pain and loss and on hope for better days. They talked and talked and talked.

Bill stepped out of the doorway of Kindred Spirit. He loved working in the shop but the continual smell of incense could sometimes affect his sinuses and so, every so often, when there were no customers, he would step outside and just stand in the doorway, surveying the precinct and the numerous empty stalls which stood like headstones in a retail graveyard.

But today, he glanced over at the chatty benches. 'Bloody daft idea,' he had always thought, 'they hardly ever get used.'

And, indeed, today the only person sat there was a young scruffy guy, quite overweight, pimply and bespectacled.

Weirdly though, it looked as if the young guy was chatting away to himself. Having a right old conversation to thin air.

Bill pondered on the terrible curse of loneliness for a while and then, with one last inhalation of incense-free air, he went back into the shop.

Revenge

VERONICA SCOTTON

Her eyes were open but expressionless. She had his attention as soon as she floated into the bar. His eyes squinted at her as if looking at the sun and didn't move away from her as he ordered from the bar, looking past the barman.

Bile rose from his stomach as he appraised her. "Just look at her, so sure of herself, so confident that men will be drawn to her. It was a woman like her that had led him astray, into the hands of the law, into the hands of the kingpin in jail. He'd spent 15 years sharing a cell at the mercy of a man who had nothing to lose, and it was all down to a bitch, just like that one.

She walked to the bar and was served her usual drink without having to say a word, the staff recognised her, and were puzzled, she couldn't be drawn into conversation, was always immaculate and always alone. With her looks, she could have had anyone she wanted but she cut dead with a look or a word each wannabe with the personality and the money to show her a good time. She just sipped her martini slowly, seeming hardly to look away from her glass.

He made his way towards her, in no doubt that he would not be able to persuade her to leave with him, he would wait outside. Perhaps he could get her inebriated first. "Are you alright love?" She didn't acknowledge that she had seen or heard him. "Are you waiting for someone?" Slowly she turned her eyes in his is general direction and said "No." He carried on talking and when the waiter asked him if he wanted another drink, he answered, "Yes a pint, a whisky chaser and whatever the lady is drinking."

The waiter looked in her direction and asked, "Are you OK miss? Is he bothering you?" Without lifting her head, she replied again, "No."

At the end of the evening, as the barman called for last orders, she stood up and walked elegantly towards the door, he hastily knocked back his chaser and followed her, she walked outside alone along the dimly lit streets, her six inch stilettoes tapping on the pavements. He had envisaged jumping into a taxi after her, or dragging her into an alley, he couldn't believe how easy she was making it for him. He decided to follow at a distance and wait for an opportunity as she walked away from the drinkers straggling in the directions of homes or jumping into taxis to nightclubs. She turned down an unadopted, unlit road that he knew led towards the canal "Was this woman insane? She was asking for trouble"

He quickened his pace, looking around him to see if anyone was watching him, but he was alone. He couldn't see her, but she couldn't have gone far in those shoes, there were no turn offs. He trotted towards the canal and as his eyes became accustomed to the darkness, he saw her outline in the pale moonlight, walking along the towpath, sauntering as if she was window shopping.

He began to remember the other woman. The one with the looks and the style, he remembered her laugh, the way she would look at him over her shoulder with love in her eyes, he remembered her soft sweet-smelling skin, her long shining hair. He knew he had been punching above his weight, why would someone like her love someone like him? His insecurities had begun to nibble at his self-esteem, he began to imagine what she was doing while he was working and harass her with questions, trying to trip her up and trick her into divulging, the other boyfriends that she must surely have had. She pitied his anxiety and tried to prove to him how much she loved and cared about him but grew frustrated when he drilled her about her boss, questioned the conversations she had with friends and made jealous remarks if she so much as looked in the direction of anyone of the opposite sex.

It was her fault, that he had felt this way, it had not been his fault that one evening in a drunken rage he had throttled her as she lied to him once more about not having eyes for anyone but him. How could that be true?

He was getting closer to the sauntering woman; he imagined the things that he would do to her before he slit her throat and threw her into the canal. Unlike her tapping shoes, his well-worn trainers made little noise and she appeared unaware of his presence.

Suddenly she turned to face him, a gun in her hand. "Hello Joe! you don't recognise me, do you?"

"What, - No, - Who are you?"

"I'm Nichola!" He wracked his brain to remember a Nichola.

"Rachael was my lovely big sister."

"Rachael! He had almost forgotten her name. For 15 years he had thought of her only as The Bitch.

His memory struggled to picture the scruffy little girl, with grazed knees and teeth missing that had sometimes tagged along with them during their early courtship, before his insecurities had turned his head.

The woman before him, with the platinum blonde hair and impeccable clothes bore no resemblance to that child, but her voice echoed in his brain, with the same nuances as his lover. Memories that had laid dormant floated into his consciousness. The bike rides, the picnics, the back row of the cinema, the laughter.

He wasn't sober, he couldn't think straight, this was all wrong, he had a knife in his hand, it would have been so easy.

"Get into the canal" she said.

"What? No, I can't. I can't swim."

"That would be even better, but I know you are lying." She cocked the gun and pointed at his heart, then slowly let it move down his body "Where would you like the first bullet?"

Automatically, his hands flew to cover his body and she saw the knife. She smiled and said, "I thought this would be so difficult, I promised myself that I would make you pay, but I wasn't sure that I could go through with it. But now it's self-defence"

He began to back up away from her, the bullet that shot through his shoe relieving him of his toes, took him back to the torture that he had endured at the hands of the kingpin. "I'll count to three then it will be your dick." He looked at the dark water, perhaps he could escape, he wouldn't have to swim far in this darkness, he turned and jumped as far as he could. The water was freezing, his winter coat heavy and dragging him under. Painfully treading water, he shrugged it off, shivering. "Go on then swim away" The woman taunted him. "My beautiful sister loved you and because she did, I loved you too. I've had to grow up without her, our parents died while you lived in the comfort of the prison, I've waited for this moment. Tell me why you killed her."

For the first time in years, he faced the truth. It wasn't her fault, she had done nothing wrong, the only mistake she had made was believing in him.

He shook his head as hot tears flowed down his freezing cheeks. He tried to swim but he had no strength, his body began to feel hot, he felt sleepy, he dreamed that he was swimming as he slowly sank to the bottom where he lay among shopping trolleys and dead cats.

Her shiny blond wig followed him down, along with the Saint Laurent shoes and Michael Costello dress. Out of the Versace handbag came trainers and jeans. The woman with the long brown hair and luminous, expressive green eyes would not have been recognised as the one that had been waiting for Joe to come into his old local since the day he had been released from prison.

Somebody

Nobody seemed bother
Nobody seemed to care
Everybody walked on by
Left him lying there

Nobody seemed to bother
Nobody seemed to care
Everybody walked on by
Left her lying there

Nobody seemed to bother
Nobody seemed to care
Everybody walked on by
Left me lying there

Nobody seemed to bother
Nobody seemed to care
Everybody walked on by
Will they leave you lying there?

WARREN DAVIES

The Cloak of Night

DAVID LOCKLEY

The moon was unusually bright that night, casting a silvery sheen on the quiet street.

'I can't believe you talked me into doing this' Yasmin's voice was hushed but still seemed loud in the nocturnal silence. Britain was enjoying the unseasonably mild Spring of 2020 and yet, at the same time, was traumatised by the recent covid lockdown.

'I've already told you how grateful I am' replied Duncan. 'And anyway, we're here now. No backing out'. He looked at his young colleague and tried to convey gratitude in his eyes.

'I don't know why we need to go to this much trouble for a mobile phone' said Yasmin as she retrieved the bunch of keys from her pocket.

Ever since lockdown, Duncan had fretted about the mobile phone he had left in his desk drawer on the day they were all hurriedly ejected from the office building.

'I told you, I need it for a million reasons and I can't afford a new one. Not on my wage.' Yasmin was on a slightly higher grade than him and he rarely missed an opportunity to comment on it. But at least it meant that he had a friend who had keys to get back into the abandoned office.

Yasmin fumbled through those keys now until she found the one that opened the front door of the office building. Duncan winced slightly as it creaked open. There was nobody in the street at 2am but he still felt wary and edgy.

Yasmin nipped through the open door to quickly disable the alarm. Duncan followed her into the dark hallway and closed the door behind them.

There was a bank of light switches next to the alarm but they didn't switch them on. The moonlight shone through the many windows to lend the interior a creepy luminosity and they knew that the less attention they drew to themselves, the better.

'Well, come on then,' whispered Yasmin, 'the sooner we get that stupid phone, the sooner we can get out of here'.

The main office was on the first floor so, with exaggerated care, they both ascended the stone steps of the stairwell. Even though they knew they were alone, there was something about the still, chilly atmosphere of the dark abandoned building that seemed to demand furtiveness.

In a hushed voice, Yasmin said 'Just imagine if Geoff could see us now. He'd have a blue fit.'

Duncan grimaced at the mention of his manager's name, as he always did. Nobody liked the swaggering arrogance of the flash little dictator but Duncan knew that Geoff reserved his keenest barbs and cruellest put-downs just for him. The rest of the office staff were fully aware of the particular toxicity of the relationship between Duncan and Geoff, which seemed to make it worse.

They emerged at the top of the stairwell to see the silhouettes of the desks, lined up like moonlit soldiers, guarding the long office space.

'Have you still got that torch?' Yasmin asked. He fumbled in his pocket to produce the small torch that they barely needed. The beam cut through the silvery gloom like a pale intruder and danced in the air until it illuminated Duncan's own desk at the bottom of the office.

They both crept down the office where Duncan directed the torch beam to the top drawer of his desk pedestal. He opened it and shone the torch beam inside.

'No...' he exclaimed as he rummaged in the drawer, scrabbling through pens and random items of stationery.

'No, no, no, it has to be here.' Panic flared in Duncan's mind as he realised the mobile phone was no longer where he had left it.

'I never put it anywhere else.' he said. He started to turn to Yasmin in confusion and to apologise for her wasted trip.

Her scream shattered the silence like a brick through a mirror.

Her wild, terrified eyes were fixed on the shadowy space under the desk. With a shaking hand, Duncan directed the torch beam there.

The corpse was shoved unceremoniously into the tight space, the knees pulled up to the chin, the face slack in death, eyes bulging, tongue protruding from blue lips. The face that belonged to Geoff.

'Oh my God' gasped Duncan. The quivering torchlight could just pick out bruising on the throat. The victim had clearly been strangled.

128

Yasmin had stopped screaming but was breathing so heavily, she was in danger of hyperventilating. Duncan turned to her and their eyes met, wide, terrified and panic-stricken.

'We have to go to the police. We have to tell them.' she said, her voice trembling and close to tears.

Despite the shock, a sudden moment of cold, clarity invaded Duncan's mind.

'Wait, Yas. Slow down. We need to think about this.'

'What is there to think about, Duncan?' she shouted. 'He's dead. We've got to tell them.'

She fumbled in her pocket and produced her mobile phone. Just as she focused on it, Duncan dashed it from her hand. They heard it skittering across the floor and into the darkness.

'What the hell do you think you're doing?' she shrieked.

Duncan had spent months sending texts to friends and colleagues, describing his burning hatred of Geoff and just what he would like to do to him. Using the phone that was now missing.

'Listen, Yas. Everybody knows how much I hated him. The police will never believe I had nothing to do with this.'

Yasmin's face was a picture of outrage.

'But we have to, Dunc. We have to report this.'

With that, she started to run towards the stairwell. His mind filled with panic, Duncan chased after her.

'Yas.' he shouted as he caught up with her, grabbing her upper arm and spinning her towards him. Even in the gloom, the look of fear and surprise was clear to see on the young woman's face as she lost her centre of gravity and toppled backwards.

Her arms flailed and almost grabbed the bannister but then, with an awful inevitability, her body plummeted down the stairwell, thumping and thudding down the hard, stone steps. The final thud was accompanied by a sickening crunching sound which seemed as loud and as shocking as her earlier scream.

Duncan stood for several seconds, his heart pounding violently in his chest and his breath coming in ragged gasps.

He was dimly aware of the cold sweat that had broken out all over him as he descended the stairwell. He found Yasmin's body in a crumpled heap, her head at an impossible angle. He didn't need to feel for a pulse to know that she was dead.

No-one expected to come across a body in an empty building, and now there were two. And nobody would believe that he was innocent.

There was a space under the stairwell, lost in even darker shadows than the rest of the hallway.

Working entirely on impulse, he bundled the still warm body of his deceased friend under the stairwell until it couldn't be seen. At least, while the indiscriminate cloak of night was still concealing the grim truth.

He paused for a few seconds to try and slow his breathing and heart rate, and then he slipped through the door and out into the silent street.

It felt surreal to let himself in through his own front door and into the cosy confines of his own house after the dramatic events of the night. He still lived with his parents but he knew they would be fast asleep. In fact, he could hear a faint snoring coming from their room.

With a care that defied his fevered state of mind, he ascended the stairs and let himself into his room. He flicked the switch and blinked in the sudden flood of light.

He had only taken a few steps towards his bed when he suddenly stopped. His already beleaguered heart felt like it would burst through his chest.

There, on his bedside table, sat the black oblong of his mobile phone. The phone that his brain had convinced him he had left in his desk The phone that was full of texts that would implicate him in the murder of his manager.

It was then, with a realisation that froze the blood in his veins, that his subconscious mind vomited up the terrible truth. The last few moments as they cleared the office on that final day before lockdown. The awkwardness as all the staff left, leaving only Duncan and the hated Geoff, who took that opportunity to launch yet another verbal assault, describing Duncan's incompetence and worthlessness in no uncertain terms. And the sudden impulsive moment when Duncan finally snapped and launched himself at his tormentor, his hands closing around his victim's throat.

The memories had submerged into the black depths of his mind, like a pebble in a deep lake. Except for one thing. The conviction that he had to go back to retrieve the phone that he had never lost. The phone that had been sat on his bedside table in full view the whole time, which his horrified mind had hidden from his sight, thus forcing him to return to the office to confront the reality of his actions in defiance of his conscious mind's attempts to shield him from the truth.

It took only a few seconds for the last vestiges of his sanity to fly from his mind like a startled bird. His head seemed to fill with the banshee howls of madness. Or were they police sirens?

Politics and The Qatar World Cup

CHRIS VICKERS

Talking About My Generation reporter Chris shares his opinions on the Qatar World Cup, his thoughts sparked by attending a creative workshop in Manchester.

I was in the audience at the National Football Museum on November 8, 2022, for their ninth Football Writing Festival where there was a nuanced debate about the upcoming Qatar World Cup.

The debate was hosted by BBC's Amber Sandhu and featured distinguished panellists David Conn, *The Guardian*; Matt Slater, *The Athletic*; Steve Cockburn, *Amnesty International* and Dr Heather Dichter from De Montfort University.

There was reference back to the extraordinary voting that awarded the 2018 competition to Russia, despite their incursion into Crimea, and 2022 to Qatar, a tiny country smaller than Yorkshire, with no football tradition.

However, given that it is the wealthiest *per capita* country in the world, this may have proved of crucial significance! Matt Slater told us that, "most of the voting committee never even read the Qatar Bid Book (700 pages) which made no reference to the large-scale human rights abuses, or of the welfare of the construction workers."

Sep Blatter has blamed Michel Platini for switching his vote from USA to Qatari and swaying others after an infamous lunch at the Élysée Palace. Platini attended along with President Sarkozy and the Emir of Qatar.

As a result of this, the Qatari's bought French fighter jets for $14.6 billion, and made strategic investments including Sarkozy's favourite football team Paris St Germaine.

"Geopolitics and corruption are always at play when awarding countries either the Olympics or the World Cup," said Professor Dichter and cited even the first World Cup in Uruguay, when they used their leverage as Olympic champions to secure the rights. We marvelled at the Argentinian ticker-tape finals featuring Mario Kempe's *et al* but disregard the nationals who were 'disappeared.'

China won the winter Olympics despite human rights abuses, and German corruption in 2006 involving Franz Beckenbauer was egregious;

the success of the finals in 2006 which introduced fan zones for the first time, however, meant that the corruption was overlooked.

Sep Blatter said: "We go to new lands. The Middle East and Arabic world have been waiting a long time. So I'm a happy president when we talk about the development of football." New lands referred presumably to enlarged TV audiences and commercial opportunities.

In Qatar there was genuine excitement and pride in winning the hosting rights and it represents a four-week window for a nation to project a global image to the rest of the world of its history and culture.

Qatar is unpopular with neighbouring countries and hosting the finals provides them with a defence mechanism as they negotiate and interact with countries worldwide.

Overall some 1.1 million construction workers were deployed not only to build nine new football stadiums but also infrastructure of new port, railways, hotels and roads which would be managed by multi-national blue-chip architects and builders.

Those workers were from places such as India, Nepal and Pakistan and wore blue overalls in 43 C temperatures doing manual work, while professionals, such as David Conn, researching for the world cup, were advised not to set foot outside due to the insufferable heat and were chauffeured from air-conditioned place to place.

According to Amnesty International hundreds of workers have perished but the Qatari Supreme Committee state the figure of deaths to be around thirty-seven, with only three due to direct stadium fatalities. They disregard people who died offsite due to heat exhaustion, heart attacks or stress which they deemed to be natural causes.

Although progress has been painstakingly slow Amnesty International report that Qatar has implemented a legal minimum wage of around $250 per month plus accommodation and food, which could be much higher given the wealth of the nation. It is the first country in the region to do so, however.

Migrant workers usually have to pay agency fees to get work in Qatar and if things go badly they can be worse off than before as they have an outstanding loan to pay back; there is now a $750 fee refund, though it applies to merely two per cent of workers presently, and it seems more ethical recruitment agencies are required.

Tickets are 97 per cent sold and the games are fast approaching (Nov 2022). Fan zones are in place but at premium costs.

The BBC and Gary Lineker are allegedly prepared to be outspoken and refer to human rights issues and Gareth Southgate said when Qatar told people to focus on only the football. "Frankly, I'll choose if I'm going to speak or not and I'm pretty sure the players will as well."

Amnesty says that it is essential that focus be retained after the finals finish to maintain social progress in the country. Let's hope that this is what happens, for as David Conn said: "When the action starts the magic happens," and it would be wonderful if football proved to be a catalyst towards a free society.

Other Publications by SWit'CH

My Life and Other Misadventure   ISBN 978-1-326-60665-7

By Alan Rick

A collection of humorous and poignant nostalgic reminiscences covering Alan's early school years in the war to national service in Egypt. Alan looks askance at the society of the day with a wry, knowing, smile.

Switch On, Write On, Read On   ISBN 978-1-326-73048-2

Approx. 200 page the first showcase of the group's creativity. Containing nearly sixty humorous, whimsical, thought-provoking, ironic, and eclectic writing.

A Write Good Read   ISBN 978-0-244-73623-1

Tales from Swinton and Salford; the Wigan train and around the world drawing on the experiences and interests of the group. Modern telecoms and IT feature, so do the Ten Commandments and seven dwarfs. Historical pieces range from the industrial revolution to individual childhood memories.

Peterloo People   ISBN 978-0-244-18472-8

A potpourri of passions gives the reader the chance to walk in those shoes to the peaceful protest, the actions on the day and shameful reaction afterwards. But the focus is not only on the victims; the perspectives of the authorities and militia are treated with sympathy and criticism in due turn – and there's even a wry tale of hope and salvation for a pariah in the guise of a government spy.

The Taste of Teardrops   ISBN 978-0-244-26569-4

A Novel by Judith Barrie.

A gripping psychological thriller set in a sleepy seaside town on The Solway Firth. It's 1981 and a young woman settles into her cosy new home believing that she had found peace and tranquillity after a painful marriage break-up.

But there are mysteries. Who is the woman upstairs? And who is the irresistibly attractive man who visits her? Susan is unaware of the nightmare of pain and deceit he will draw her into, driving her to the very edge of her sanity.

Memories Unlocked   ISBN 9798570919617

These childhood reminiscences of localities now gone, holidays, school, nature notes, plane crashes, sex education and walking home after dancing form part of the mischief, mayhem and misadventures of our young lives. Drawn from the experiences of SWit'CH writers in their formative years.

The Big Switch   ISBN : 9798644090433

A collection of short stories in large print format for readers with a visual impairment such as Macular Degeneration or Glaucoma.

'The Big Switch' is a compilation of extracts from some of the group's previously published works. Designed for easy reading.

Selected Memories   ISBN 9798598323212

This choice of writers' recollections taken from Memories Unlocked follows on from *The Big Switch*, which was produced for those with a visual impairment, with a font developed by RNIB.

The book is easy to handle. Big letters on low contrast paper make it an easy read and a 'page turner' in the literal sense.

A Pain in the Bum   ISBN: 9798590032099

Veronica Scotton

The author's words say it all "I was so very fortunate, not to have to face my cancer alone. Whenever I began to feel overwhelmed, the rock who is my husband was by my side. My children and grandchildren lifted my spirits by being positive about the whole thing and my siblings and friends with their humour, often black humour gave me the best medicine."

Time of the Virus   ISBN: 9798541841855

Sylvia Edwards

The personal reflection written during the 2020/2021 Coronavirus pandemic. Complemented with Sylvia's own artworks, poetry and stories.